TO OUR CHILL

C000253118

Thank you
To those who read the first versions
giving feedback and encouragement.

Especially Michael and Fiona
Liz and Sara

And to Ken Dawson of Creative Covers.
For helping me make my cover design a reality.

The words that the Angels speak are inspired by The Gospel
of The Essenes, as translated by Edmond B Szekely.
The C. W. Daniel Co Ltd Saffron Walden.
(Words in italics are direct quotes).

*There are questions around Szekelys' source material for these
translations, but I will leave that for the academics. To me the words
are Heaven Sent; Perhaps there was an Angel whispering in his ear.*

The moral right of Miranda Bruce to be identified as the author of this
work has been asserted by her in accordance with the Copyright, Designs
and Patent Act 1988.

CONTENTS

Chapter   **Page**

The Crystal and the Stars

Chapter 1

A Disturbed Night

Robin goes to bed as usual, at nine. She had a busy day, helping Mum plant seeds in the greenhouse, so she only reads her book for a short while before she switches off the light, turns to her comfortable sleeping position and falls into a deep sleep.

Something wakes her. A dark shape rushes across the rectangle of light on the wall by her bed and her heart beats faster. She sits up, to rouse herself from the confusion of half sleep. There's nothing there, but her bedroom door has swung open letting in the light from the landing. She gets out of bed to close the door and hears the sound of raised voices coming from down stairs.

Robin makes her way down a small staircase to the door at the bottom that leads straight into the sitting room. The door has been left off the latch and the sound of her parents arguing had travelled up the stairs and into her room. She pushes open the door and cries out. "Stop fighting. You're letting the dark in. I can feel it in the house."

Her father turns his head and looks over the back of the sofa. "Stop being so dramatic Robin. Shut the door and go back to bed. Parents argue sometimes. It's nothing to worry about."

Robin gets back into bed but it still feels like there's something in the shadows, so she pulls the covers over her head hoping it won't notice her if she pretends to be asleep. She can still hear the muffled murmur of her parent's voices. Sometimes raised and then very quickly hushed again. That; and the thrumming of the moth, caught inside the landing lampshade, its shadow sweeping across the walls.

It feels like an age before she can settle but eventually, she does drift back to sleep.

Animals at Dawn

Robin wakes at dawn and can't bear to stay in bed any longer. She pulls on some jeans and a jumper and very quietly slips out of the house.

The night is still starry in the deep blue sky, as it fades into the early morning light. Whenever she's troubled, Robin finds comfort walking through the fields behind their land. In the sound of the wind, as it swirls through the barley, she hears voices whispering, "We love you." And she runs on down to the sea with the light of a new day dawning.

When she reaches the top of a low cliff she stands and looks across the sea. The waves stretch her heart out towards the horizon; and the sea breeze fills her with joy and excitement; and she feels as free as all the wildness around her: As free as the gulls spiralling overhead.

Robin often likes to get up just as dawn is breaking. It's the best time to meet wildlife. The night animals are on their way home and the day animals are just waking up. At this time of the year they're all occupied with preparing for their young, too busy finding food to take much notice of Robin. She knows where the barn owls nest each year; and where the bats make their home in the tree hollow; and which of the deer's beds were slept in that night. They look like large nests of flattened grass in the field margins; and she knows the hare field and the badger sets and fox dens; and the bend in the river where the otters rear their pups and water voles vanish, quick as a flash into their cool, river bank tunnels. Nearer to home there's a place at the back of the spinach patch where the mother hedgehog disappears into the hedge, in the early morning.

On her way home, Robin spends time down by the hollow oak where the vixen has her cubs in her den beneath the roots. Lying on her stomach on cool leaves and twigs, Robin hides behind a large fallen branch. She's been waiting for the cubs to be old enough to come out and play and finally, today, her patience is rewarded when first one and then three more, tumble out into the emerging light. They're still very young and the mother only allows them out for a short while, tottering about, sniffing and trembling, and it feels like a good omen after the night she had, so she makes her way home in a much better mood.

Robin opens the yard gate and can see Mum in the barn, putting together boxes of vegetables to sell at the roadside stall. Their best trade is with people returning from trips to the coast.

Her mum looks up from what she's doing. "There you are! I was hoping you'd help me with this, but you're too late now. You'd better see to the animals first and then you can get your own breakfast. When you've finished your chores, I'd like you to write that essay we talked about yesterday, and then help Peter. Every thing's running late today."

Her parents have to work hard but they find enough time to home school Robin and she helps out by looking after the animals and working in the gardens for pocket money.

Mum seems a bit tense and Robin thinks it's probably because of the night before. Her parents are no longer happy with each other. They had started to argue a few months ago and since then Robin's been spending more time away, exploring the countryside around the village. It's difficult for her. Even though it's her parents who aren't getting along, it feels like she's the one who's getting more and more left out. They had all been so close before. She loves her mum, but when her parents argue she often finds herself secretly on her dad's side. Something has happened that they haven't told her about and her mum has become more and more irritable, so Dad spends longer outside working, which Robin knows only makes things worse.

"Where's Dad?"

"He's gone to London for a few days."

"I didn't know he was going."

"No, nor did I." Mum slams a box down on the bench and starts rummaging through some invoices in a fluster. Robin decides she'd better leave it at that so makes her way to the shed to get the food for the animals.

An Awkward Supper

It's been two hours since Mum told Robin that her dad would be back in time for supper. Robin's sitting on the box seat under the window, reading a book, but mostly she's staring at the rain bouncing off the concrete in the yard and running along the bottom of the wall as a little stream, forming a muddy puddle at the gate. "Finally!"

Dad's headlights come down the track. Robin races to the front door to welcome him in out of the rain. She opens the door as he gets out of the car; the wind blowing rain into the porch.

"Dad! How was your stay? I didn't know you were going to London."

"I'll tell you about it later sweetheart. Just let me get through the door, I'm dying for a cup of tea. Where's your mum?"

And that was it. He and Mum are in the office talking and it seems an age before they come out, and then he goes upstairs while Mum finishes preparing supper and Robin lays the table.

Robin can sense the tension between them as they sit down for supper. They eat the first course saying very little. Robin tries a couple of times to start a conversation about London with Dad but he puts her off each time, so she gives in to the silence.

Mum gets up from the table. "I'll go and get the pudding."

Dad pores himself a glass of wine and watches her leave the room as he takes a sip. "Robin, your mum and I have been talking and I need to tell you about some changes we're going to have to make." He pauses to put his glass down on the mat, lingering over it, running his finger around the rim while he gathers his thoughts. "You know we've been going through some difficult times lately, and I'm afraid the sums just aren't adding up. I've found a good job in London and I can stay in Grans' flat there."

Robin tries to protest but he doesn't give her a chance.

"Now don't say anything yet, I have quite a lot to tell you first."

Mum comes in and puts the pudding in front of them, then sits down beside Robin and takes her hand.

"We've decided that we can just about manage to keep the place. With Pete and the weekend helpers; and with the income from this new job I've found; and if Mum can find a part time job for a while. Now it means you're going to have to go to school. I need you to be grown up about this Robin. You want us to keep the place, don't you?"

"Yes, but once I've started school there'll be no going back, will there? I just know it. And how long do you need to work in London for? Are you going to come back to us?"

There's a look between her parents at this question. Robin doesn't quite understand it, but it's enough for her to know that she's not going to get a straight answer.

4

Robin takes a spoonful of apple crumble just because she doesn't know what to do or say, but she regrets it because she can't swallow it. In the end she has to put it back on the spoon, from her mouth. She sits fighting back the tears, looking down at the horrid half chewed mess in her bowl. Her mother's saying something but she can't pay attention to it. "May I go to my room now?"

"Of course, if you need to, but I'd like to talk some more, when you've had a chance to take it all in. I'm sure you'll have more questions later."

Mum's still holding her hand and can't quite bring herself to let it go. As if somehow that can make everything all right. It irritates Robin slightly and she just wants to get away.

"I'm so sorry." Dad says it almost as a whisper, looking into his glass, knowing that it won't really help.

Falling asleep is hard. Too many thoughts tossing her about in her bed. The last thing she remembers is the uncertainty about whether her dad will come back to live with them. Eventually she sleeps and falls into a dream.

She's spiralling through the sky on the back of a raven, gliding above green fields and dark blue sea. They cross over a field with a horse galloping beneath them, leading them towards the branches of an enormous tree. As they get closer Robin can see through the earth, to her vixen, curled around her sleeping pups in a hollow beneath its roots. The raven turns upwards, up and up and up to clear the towering branches and from among the leaves, a strange music, woven from many voices, whispers secrets into the wind.

Chapter 2

The Runaway

Robin waits until her mum finally goes to work on the stall. She'd had another restless night. After that awful supper, her parents had spent more nights arguing, but she still hadn't been able to hear the words clearly enough to understand what it was really about. She's finding the tension between them unbearable. She's always in the middle and at the same time, always left out.

This morning Robin got up with the certainty that the only thing to do was to run away. As soon as her mum leaves, she packs a rucksack with a change of clothes; some food; a lighter she finds in the sitting room draw; an old saucepan and spoon; torch; water; a sleeping bag and the money she earned working with Peter Pike picking lettuces in the poly-tunnel. She's not sure about her phone, then decides to take it but to keep it turned off.

It's an odd feeling closing the door behind her. She can't quite believe that running away means she won't be coming back. She takes in everything in sharpened focus. The door, and the way the dry mud is cracked around the bottom of the step, and the dandelion that ought to be weeded out.

The first part of her journey doesn't feel very different than any other day when she would set off for a walk. All the roads and short cuts are familiar. Then she gets to the dual carriageway where she would normally turn back. She stands on the roadside daring herself to go on. Cars race by and she just stands there, anchored to the spot. Caught in the moment. She's not really certain that this is what she wants to do.

Everything's changing. Her mum's looking for a part time job and Robin's going to have to go to school. She hates the idea of going to school. She thinks they'll want to change her somehow, like domesticating an animal and anyway she doesn't really feel comfortable with people. Every time she says anything it comes out clumsy and awkward, somehow wrong as soon as it comes out of her mouth and not at all what she's really thinking. It gives her a worried, uncomfortable feeling when she speaks.

So she ends up not speaking at all, and that isn't any better. She finds it so much easier with animals; they know who you are without having to explain yourself.

She's standing on the side of the dual carriageway, worrying about how long it will take before Mum realises, she isn't coming back. Desperately hoping that if her parents see how much it means to her, they won't turn her world upside-down. She looks down at her feet. There's a little eruption in the tarmac where a blade of grass is pushing its way through. "Is it the grass that got stronger with the passing of time, or did the tarmac get weaker?" Then she realises something about never giving up, some law of nature that's on your side as long as you keep trying. In the end she just starts walking along the dual carriageway while thinking about the blade of grass, so she forgets to worry about which direction to take and after a few yards she's walking with a spirit of adventure.

Robin eats Marmite sandwiches she made for lunch and stops for a short while to look at a swarm of tiny red spiders spreading out across the white concrete of the pavement edging. It's a humid day. A smell of electricity is in the air and way out on the horizon, a yellowish haze hangs under a bank of grey clouds, with the occasional roll of distant thunder.

She's walking along the footpath that runs parallel to the bypass, with cars flashing noisily past. The wild verge full of yellow and black striped caterpillars, devour ragwort in the long grasses.

Robin's beginning to feel a bit exposed on the main road, a girl alone. She's worried that it might look a bit odd as it's getting late. She doesn't want to draw attention to herself and she needs to find shelter if the clouds turn to rain. The opportunity comes with a field gate and a track that drops below a small hill where she can just make out the roof of what looks like a barn. She stands for a moment and watches the cloud bank engulf an early star in the grey light. Then she turns and climbs over the gate and starts off down to the barn. With a flash of lightning the first drops of rain begin to fall. Each drop releasing the scent of earth as it hits the warm, dried mud on the track.

The Barn

Robin reaches the barn and looks around. There's no one about. Further down the track is a derelict looking farmhouse. She's startled by the loud "caw" of a large bird. Sitting on the corner of the barn roof is a raven. She stares up at it, enjoying the light, cool rain on her face. She's never seen a raven in real life before. She knows crows. They're the noisy neighbours that roost in untidy, twiggy, tangled nests woven into the tops of tall trees at the boundary of their land; and she knows jackdaws. They fly over the house each day at teatime. Passing over in small flocks, calling to each other with their funny, nasal chatter.

This is definitely a raven. It's big, with a long, chiselled bill. It looks down at her with an impersonal gaze, turning its head from side to side, looking through one eye and then the other; then hunches its wings and shakes off the fine rain.

Robin watches as it takes flight, and as it stretches out its wings, light from the setting sun, pierces through the cloud line and lights up a blue fluorescence in the glistening blackness of the raven's feathers.

The barn seems little used but there's still the heavy smell of animals. There's hay and straw, slimy and dark under a hole in the roof. In one corner an oily, faded tarpaulin full of frayed holes, has been thrown over oil drums and remnants of rusted machinery. Robin is very hungry. She has some cheese and potatoes and decides to cook herself some supper.

They often make fires at home. She's usually put in charge of the fire when she helps her mother scything down bramble or pruning hedges. It's one of her favourite jobs because Buster their staffie comes too.

When her mother can't pull free a particularly stubborn branch, Buster loves to get involved. He'll get hold of the end of the branch and happily tug it out, growling to himself. The more stubborn a branch, the more he enjoys the challenge, until with tugs that shake the whole hedge it gives way to his powerful jaws and shoulders. Then he'll drag it over to Robin and lay at her feet until she's ready to wrestle it away from him, to throw it onto the fire.

She misses Buster already and wishes she could have brought him

with her. Robin usually enjoys working alongside her mum.
She makes jobs fun and notices when Robin does something well.
Dad taught her how to build a fire properly, making sure the ground
is clear of anything that might catch alight; taking note of which way
the wind's blowing.

The barn is very tall with a corrugated iron, porch roof, running
along the front. Robin clears an area of ground down to the concrete
area beneath it. She finds some dry hay and splinters of wood that
brake easily from an old, dry, rotten plank. The rest of the plank she
brakes over her knee, for larger pieces. She lights the kindling and
gradually adds larger pieces, making sure the fire doesn't get too big
and finally lays two flat pieces side by side, with a gap in-between to
put the saucepan on. Her penknife blade is too short to slice the
potatoes so they end up as strangely shaped chunks and there isn't
much water so she only just covers the potatoes in the pan.

When she's sure that the saucepan won't fall over, Robin goes to
look for more fire wood. The rain's still light, so the wood under the
hedge beside the barn is dry. She's back just in time to save the
potatoes. All the water has boiled away and they've stuck to the
bottom, but at least they haven't burnt. The potatoes are still slightly
hard and taste of wood smoke but she finds it a curiously pleasing
taste, warm and filling with the cheese.

It's growing darker and Robin's feeling anxious. Her mum was
working at the roadside stall and Robin had been relying on her
thinking that she was gardening with Pete. She thought that the note
she'd left in the bathroom (Mum always has a shower first when she
comes in) would be reassuring enough. "I'm OK. Just had to get
away for a while. Love you. Robin." But her mum must be home
now and Robin can feel that the note isn't reassuring at all. She can
see in her mind's eye her mum, standing there with the note in her
hand and can feel what she'd be feeling, senses the house spinning
round and round her, phoning Robin's dad as she worries about what
to do.

Robin's first impulse is to get up and run straight back to them, but
it's pouring with rain now and dark and when she stops to think
about it, she still can't bear to go home, to the arguing and
everything that's changing. She thinks again about what it is she's
doing. She hadn't thought beyond setting her feet on the road and
seeing where it led; but how is she going to shop without being
recognised? How is she going to eat once her money runs out?

Are things so terrible at home that she would do this to her parents? But she hasn't run away to get back at her parents. She hasn't run away because they're terrible. Why don't they understand that she just can't face losing the world she loves so much? Robin's feeling horrible. One moment she's feeling she's being awful to her parents and the next moment she's thinking that no one understands her or cares how she feels about the changes they're making.

The Jewellery Box

It's late and cold and Robin puts on her coat and huddles miserably into her sleeping bag. She sits, leaning against the door frame, facing her small fire, close enough to the wood pile to throw more on when needed. Folding her arms around her knees she rests her forehead on them, trying to untangle her feelings. After a while she gets up to check the fire, poking it with a stick to bring it back to life. When she sits back down, she puts her hands in her pockets. "That's strange!" Amongst the fluff, an old dog biscuit and some sweet wrappers, is a crystal. She doesn't remember putting it in her pocket. It's about palm size and very clear, with some small chips out of the base where it must have knocked against something in the past. She found it one day in her mother's old jewellery box.

When Robin was ill, when she was younger, her mum had let her play with her odds and ends box. It was full of broken jewellery and buttons and such. She sat in bed creating landscapes on her duvet, where her knees made hills and necklaces made rivers. There were trees made out of broaches and flowers from ear rings, and there she'd found the crystal and used it in her made-up world. She hadn't thought much more about it after that. Sometime later she found it again, when she put her hand in her dressing gown pocket, and then on another day she put her hand in the pocket of her cardigan, and there it was again. Now here it is again.

The crystal grows warm as she holds it in her hand. It feels reassuring and Robin doesn't want to put it down. Sitting gazing into the fire she becomes more and more dreamy and sleepy. Looking down at the crystal it feels like it's drawing her into it, speaking to her but silent. It's in her hand and somehow all around her too, huge; then some part of her expands out into it, huge too.

10

She can feel a sensation like a deep hum, that's so soothing and holds her very still, not wanting to leave it....

Robin is standing on a small hill, in the land made of jewels that she created on her duvet. Ahead of her runs a crystal-clear stream, edged with willows of silver, leafed in green sapphires. She feels the gentle touch of a warm breeze on her face and then a voice speaks. It's not her own voice in her head. It speaks to her from somewhere else, from all around her. As she listens there is a silence between each sentence and she feels again the warmth of the breeze on her face.

"We are those who watch over you...
"We whisper to you in the barley fields and when you reach the sea, we are there with you too...
"We have many names: Angels, Guardians, Ancestors and others...
"We're always with you, helping you on life's journey...
"We're here now to help you understand, you can't run away from life. Life is a river...
"You move through life and learn, so that you can use all that you have learnt, to help you change from inside...
"So that your heart can grow bigger and bigger...
"Your heart is already bigger...
"You feel it...
"Your parents have a purpose to care for you, but you care about them too and you know that that is more important to you than your fears...
"This is your heart growing...
"This is the truth that you are feeling..."

Angel of Power

Robin opens her eyes and sees that the fire has gone out but at least she's woken up in a much better mood, full of the certainty that she's doing the right thing. She's going home. She kicks the hot embers out into the wet grass and stands in the cool air, holding the crystal in her pocket, listening to the last remnants of the rain dripping from the leaves in the hedge.

The stars are so bright they give enough light to see without the moon. She looks up at them and above her the Milky Way stretches across the sky.

Robin looks back down and has the odd sensation that she can't see properly. She's looking towards the blackness of some trees ahead of her, but there still seem to be constellations swimming in front of her eyes. She stands still trying to make out what it is that she's seeing. Within the dark there is something moving ever so slowly towards her and her stomach turns a summersault. Gradually a shape appears. It's a shape made of transparent blackness full of stars. The movement makes it easier to see the form in contrast to the denser black of the trees beyond it. It's about the same height as an elephant but twice as long; with a tail as long again; and a long neck and graceful head and looking into its eye is like looking into a distant sun. It's beautiful. It stops a little way from her and flexes two huge, glass black wings, throwing its head back with a snort and then stands very still. It takes Robin's breath away. All she can do is stand and stare. And then it speaks!

"So, you're not afraid of me?"

Robin takes a step back, but then stands her ground. "How can I be? You're so beautiful. What are you?"

"I am formed out of a thought within the mind of the great Creator. I am created by the power that flows through all forms and makes all form possible. Come child with no fear. Get on my back and I'll show you."

As soon as the creature spoke to her, Robin was no longer afraid, but she still feels apprehensive. As for getting on its back, it doesn't seem possible. It doesn't look as though this creature has any true substance. As though she'd fall straight through if she tried. She approaches it and tentatively reaches out. She can't see the surface of its body but her hand makes contact with it and it is indeed solid. It crouches down to lower itself and Robin runs her hand slowly along its neck, as she would with her pony Polly and in one fluid movement jumps up to sit astride it. The creature raises itself up to full height and Robin feels a long way from the ground. Then it leaps into the sky. Up and up and up. Out beyond the atmosphere and into space. Robin is afraid that she won't be able to breath in space but she never has to take a breath, like a fish must feel in water.

They head towards the Milky Way and as they race into the stars it calls out to her. "You see all these stars? There is a power behind the law that directs each star to form. The same power that guides you in all that you do. It's the power that flows effortlessly through everything. Can you feel it Robin?"

She can feel it. She has been riding, clinging to the star creature's neck. Now she sits up with her arms outstretched. It feels as though she is transparent, with the whole universe rushing through her. She can feel it like a constant wind through her, as they speed towards the Milky Way. With a sudden pull, they join the multitude of stars, caught in a current circling the Galaxy. They pass suns spinning their essence out into space and solar systems in the distance, like atoms, planets as electrons, circling stars at their nucleus. Far, far away are nebulas where stars are born. They are drawn further and further in. Pulled by an irresistible current, to fly a wide birth around a black hole - the great in breath at the centre of the Galaxy.

Robin is in a place where time is quite different. It could have been hours or an hour. But still. All too soon. They are back on the ground.

The creature speaks to her again. "I am the messenger of the Angel of Power, sent to remind you that power doesn't come from you. Doesn't belong to you. It comes through you as a gift: The power that is given to everyone, everything, to create Heaven out of Life. Speak these words to call upon the Angel of Power whenever you are in need." It lifts up its head and stretches out its great wings as it recites the words.

"Angel of Power.
Descend upon my Acting Body and direct all my acts."

The creature stands for a while with Robin still on its back. Its chin stretched up towards the heavens in reverence, and then lowers its body to the ground for her. She gets off, reluctantly and stands for a while with her arms around its neck. Then it raises itself up to leave.

Robin watches as the creature dissolves back into the night. As she stands, breathing in the stars, Robin feels completely a part of them. Drawn along in the same current. All burning with the same light to create this Life. It makes her feel she is strong enough not to run away and she understands better why she should go home.

She is a part of the power that created the stars and that flows through them and through her too.

Hers is just one little life amongst a glorious constellation of lives. She doesn't feel afraid to walk home in the dark. The stars are her friends and she is up in the sky with them, looking down on herself all the way.

It's the beginning of the dawn and a few early rising birds are already singing. Robin is almost back at the turn off to her village when she becomes aware of the flashing blue light coming up behind her. She's afraid at first, thinking she's in big trouble, but the policeman's very kind and takes her straight home.

Her mother opens the door. "Where have you been Robin? I've been so worried."

"I'm so sorry."

"That's alright sweetheart, we know this is hard for you," her dad says, as they all three stand, wrapped in a big hug, and she realises then that she'll never really loose her dad. The important thing is that her parents will always love her and she will always love them too.

Chapter 3

Angel of the Sun.

Robin's dad returned to London and she and her mum are doing their best to adapt to him not being around. Robin wonders if she's ever going to get used to him not being in the bathroom when she wants to use it in the morning. They used to make a race out of who could get there first.

Robin stands, looking out of her bedroom window. The Sun still low in the sky, shining straight in, a shaft of sunlight across the primrose yellow paintwork. Her thoughts are full of the experience she had with the crystal and the stars. The crystal is on the windowsill casting rainbows in the early morning light. The Sun shines onto her, warming her body and she thinks of those creatures like lizards and dragonflies that rely on the Sun to warm them, giving them heat and energy like re-charging their batteries.
Thinking of the Sun's warmth so near, yet coming from so far away, she remembers her ride with the messenger of the Angel of Power and hears it speak to her again.
"Recite these words Robin, when you open yourself to the Sun.

Angel of the Sun, enter my Solar Centre
And give the Fire of Life to my whole body."

She can feel the place just under where her ribs meet, her solar plexus, a place that is painful sometimes when she's anxious. Now her solar plexus is full of the energy of the Sun, its strength and warmth pouring into her: The fire that fuels Life. The Sun that is always drawn with a smile. Still standing in front of the widow. She closes her eyes and repeats the words.

"Angel of the Sun, enter my Solar Centre
And give the Fire of Life to my whole body."

And feels herself filled with Sunlight.

Deborah

Robin makes her way downstairs and the kitchen is full of the smell of scrambled eggs. Buster's sitting to attention by the larder door, with his most innocent, good boy face. The one he always uses when waiting to be fed and the cats are meowing and turning circles round her legs. It feels odd to see Mum sitting alone at the kitchen table, drinking tea and reading a book, trying to ignore the animals. Waiting for Robin to feed them. She collects up bowls and starts filling them.

"I don't really want to go to Deborah's party Mum."
Robin spends time with Deborah because she's the daughter of her parent's friends. They come from London to stay in their cottage some weekends and holidays. Deborah's a bit older than Robin and acts superior and bossy and Robin's not sure she really likes her. She's greedy too. Robin has been feeling more and more troubled by something that happened the other day. They'd gone together to the little corner shop. It's owned by an elderly couple, Mr. and Mrs. Stubs. The shop feels like it's probably just the same as it was when they first opened it as newlyweds, years ago. Some of the cans on the shelves look like they've been there that long too.
They bought some sweets from the pick and mix at the front of the counter. Deborah always has plenty of pocket money. When they were at the till paying, Deborah asked for some sweets from a jar on the shelves behind the counter and when Mr. Stubs turned to get the jar, Robin saw Deborah quickly take a handful of pick and mix and put them into her pocket. Robin knew it was wrong but she felt too embarrassed to say anything. Now she's upset with herself for being a coward and not doing the right thing; especially as Mr. and Mrs. Stubs have always been so kind and friendly towards her.
Her mum puts her book to one side. "But your' dad's coming down to meet us. It will give you a chance to catch up with him."
"Oh, alright but I don't want to go on spending time with Deborah."
"Why not?"
"I don't think I really like her."
Robin's mum is a bit disappointed by this. "I know she's difficult Robin but she doesn't know anyone else down here. Can't you just be a bit kinder? She's not here that often."

"But I'm afraid she's going to get me into trouble."

"Oh come on, she's not that bad."

The mood between them is getting a bit tense and Robin answers too quickly, without thinking.

"But she steals things."

"What do you mean?"

Robin hadn't meant this to come out. She hadn't wanted to involve the adults, in case things got more serious than she intended. Now she has to tell her mum the whole story.... ".... and she had plenty of pocket money so she was just being greedy."

"It seems to me people who are greedy are often trying to fill a need, a kind of hole. The sad thing is that what they're greedy for will never fill that hole, not until they understand why they're unhappy. When you're happy it doesn't matter whether you have a thing or not, does it? You're still happy any way."

They stop talking while she empties the washing machine and then she says. "You can't just pretend that nothing's happened. You know that, don't you?"

"I know but I don't know what to say to her now."

"Well, why don't you just tell her how you feel about Mr. and Mrs. Stubs?"

The scrambled eggs are making her toast soggy so Robin gets on with eating, in silence. She's trying to imagine how she's going to bring the subject up with Deborah.

Peace with the Body

Robin clears her breakfast as quickly as she can. She has an irresistible need to be outside. The door closes behind her and she steps out into the morning; and life.

Robin loves the morning chores with the animals. To her animals are so full of life. It feels like they give off energy that flows into her and makes her feel more alive too; and the work makes her feel healthy and strong; and even when the weather is bad and wet or cold or windy, she finds it exhilarating.

Robin walks over to the stable. She opens the top half of the stable door and Polly's already there, waiting to greet her.

Polly is a beautiful Welsh Cob; dark, dark brown, nearly black; with a long, creamy white mane and tail.

She has a small white blaze, slightly off centre on her forehead. Robin's dad liked to use her to pull a cart when he collected the crates of harvested vegetables from the fields. Rather her, than the big tractor that chewed up the tracks; and Polly would put all her strong heart into pulling anything for him. She's sensible and strong; and it feels like they're flying when Robin canters her.

Robin fills Polly's hay net and then crosses the yard to let out and feed the chickens and geese. They're always so excited to see her. They run along the fencing after her. She throws some grain over the ground for them while she fills their feeders, then stands back for a while watching them happily picking out the few sunflower seeds that are mixed in with the grain. Once everyone's fed, Robin rides Polly bareback up to the paddock and puts her in with the goats. Finally, she mucks out the stable and collects the eggs.

Angel of Love

Robin's dad is already at the party when she arrives with Mum. At home she used to find it reassuring that they could spend long times together, comfortable in each other's silence, while she helped him with whatever job he was doing. Sharing his private atmosphere. She forgets that he can be quite sociable too.

He's in the middle of a small group. In mid speech he just opens wide his arm to her without stopping, including her automatically, holding her close as he continues with his conversation. Not in a way that makes Robin feel his conversation is more important than saying hello to her. She knows that he just naturally feels her as a part of himself.

"Yes, but that's not the only route the road could take. There's still the land that the Church once offered."

They're talking about the new bypass; a subject that only holds her interest for a short while.

Robin decides she ought to see where Deborah is, even though she knows that Deborah has invited some friends from London. The cottage is very old but everything inside it has a cold, unlived-in newness about it.

Robin's house isn't untidy but here there's something about the exact order in everything that makes her uneasy. It makes her feel like she'd like to break something to relieve the tension. It's not a feeling she could explain to anyone else.

Robin goes upstairs and walks along the landing until she can see, through the open door, Deborah sitting on her bed in her bedroom with her friends. From that distance they have an air of the kind of confidence Robin envies. Knowing what to say, seeming at ease, having interesting and fun conversations. This worldly set from London. But when she gets close enough to hear what they're saying, she realises that the only thing they're interested in is in finding ways to criticise any one they can name, celebrity or friend, in a cruel and petty way. It makes her glad she isn't a part of them. She calls it "their should world". You should wear this; and you should talk like that; and you should behave like this; and all the "should" that you need to do to be cool enough to fit in with them. "No thanks." Not for her.

She stands in the doorway until Deborah looks up. Robin just gives a little wave and carries on walking.

A few steps away from the door she hears Deborah say. "Oh, that's just Squinty, she hangs around me all the time."

Robin knows there are children who call her Squinty. It's not that so much that bothers her. It's the "just" that was put in front of it. "Just Squinty." She does have one lazy eye and she's supposed to wear corrective glasses all the time but she only uses them as reading glasses. It's another reason why she doesn't want to go to school and saying that she always hangs around Deborah is just a cruel lie, when Robin only spends time with Deborah out of kindness.

Robin goes back along the landing and downstairs looking for her friend Bobby. She can hear the different sounds of different conversations, from different rooms. When she arrives at the kitchen the door is a little ajar. Some of the mums are talking together.

"...but it only lasted as long as it took for her to get scared and then she came running back home." It's her mother's voice.

A few of them laugh. Not an unkind laugh. The kind reserved for mothers, for the cute acts of their children. Even so, Robin knows they're talking about her and it makes her feel belittled and misunderstood. She goes on looking for Bobby. Then, she takes a turn and there he is. Standing in the hallway with his arms already outstretched, as if he knew she was coming round the corner.

Bobby is a good friend. He has Downs's syndrome and has just turned fourteen and has been in foster care most of his life. He's special too, because he has more natural love and wisdom than anyone else Robin knows.

If a guest came, he would be the first to make them feel welcome. If someone was sad, he would be the one who would give them a hug. Betty Fry, his foster mum, considers him "a gift from God" with all the love and simple understanding he brings into the house; and into the lives of the constant stream of foster children she cares for. Bobby gives Robin a huge bear hug. Just what she needs.

"Come with me, you've got to see this. Deborah's dad taught me how to use it this morning." Bobby leads her into the kitchen and past the women sitting around the kitchen table. Robin is relieved to see her mum's no longer with them.

"Look at this, you can make hot cheese sandwiches." Bobby gets on with making toasted sandwiches, describing every part of the process as he goes. Why he should wash his hands first; and how to handle a knife; and how the toaster gets really hot. Of course, Robin has seen a toasted sandwich maker before and knows how to use a knife, but she's not going to spoil his fun by letting on.

"Come on. Let's have our own picnic," and he hands the toasted sandwiches to Robin and grabs a bowl of crisps and a carton of juice and they make their way into the garden, down to the small pond beside the Weeping Willow. They sit happily eating the toasted sandwiches, spending their time together just gazing into the water and the life beneath the surface.

"Poor Deborah."

Robin can't understand what Bobby means by this. "What do you mean, poor Deborah?"

Bobby looks at her, surprised she didn't just agree with him and after a few stammers he says. "I think that every mum's little girl is like her doll when she was a little girl. I can see your mum's doll. She was the kind of doll that got carried around everywhere, getting messy in the garden and having tea parties with other dolls and teddies. Deborah's like the doll in the glass case her mum has in the hall."

Robin remembers the feeling she had when she came into the house and tries to imagine Deborah living in that atmosphere. Something suffocating and controlled. "Yes, I see what you mean. It's good of you to care about Deborah though, when she's so horrible to you." Deborah was horrible too. Called him "your Mong friend" and said that he was too ugly to be around her.

"Oh, she's just jealous. She doesn't know how to be warm and everyone wants to be warm really."

Robin's mum once suggested that Robin should try feeling sorry for the children who called her names, because people who weren't nice probably didn't have very nice lives themselves. But this was different. Bobby genuinely has nothing but sympathy for Deborah. Caring about other people is just the natural way to be for him.

"Bobby. Bobby." Betty Fry's calling from the house.

"I've got to go. I said I'd help lay out the buffet. You coming?"

"No, I think I'll stay here for a bit."

Robin sits quietly for a little longer thinking about Bobby. Surely it should be as easy as that for everyone? Why can't everyone care about people as easily as Bobby? Bobby's love comes from his ability to see when people aren't happy. He hates unhappiness. He feels it too when people are unhappy, even if they aren't very nice to him. He sees everyone as equals and just assumes that a businessman can have just as vulnerable feelings as a little boy in the playground. And he understands the healing power of simple affection.

Robin often carries the crystal with her since the night in the barn. She takes it out of her pocket while watching the setting Sun. She holds it up, turning it in her hand, looking through it from different angles. Then she feels a warm breeze on her face and the voice from the crystal lands all around her again, whispering in the shimmer of the willow leaves.

"Let your love be as the Sun that shines on all creatures of the Earth and does not favour one blade of grass for another."

Robin closes her eyes and feels a sensation of warmth in the centre of her heart. As it grows and expands the voice speaks again.

"Speak this prayer when you call to the Angel of Love.

Angel of Love,
Descend upon my feeling body and purify all my feelings."

Chapter 4

Angel of Water

Robin's mum said that she'd collect the eggs and Peter Pike offered to muck out the stable so Robin has the morning to herself. She takes a walk through the top paddock to the edge of the wood, where the stream runs through it. It's a beautiful, fresh morning; the scent of moss in the cold dew. It rained heavily during the night so the stream's running fast, with deep pools here and there.

Robin walks beside the stream, the Sun glaring bright through gaps in the trees, making it hard to see into the shade. She comes to a part of the stream where the banks are high and the water deep and dark. Cutting through the darkness a shaft of sunlight shines directly onto a water-lily. It's caught in a small whirlpool in the currents, close to the further bank of the stream. This is odd, because all the water-lilies are in the Millpond down-stream and Robin knows there are none up stream, and anyway it's too early in the year for them to flower.
She picks up a long stick and holding onto a branch, reaches across the water hoping to pull the lily back into the currents, to watch it continue on its journey. As the stick dips down into the water behind the lily there's a tug on the end of it. Robin thinks it might be tangled in some weeds so she tugs back. This time there's definitely a pull back on it, so she pulls again harder.
Robin falls backwards as a small girl lets go of the other end of the stick and comes out of the water. Her hair is as green as pond weed and her dress as yellow as water iris. She's smiling, and laughing with golden eyes and seems very excited.
"Come with me. Come with me."
There's no time to think. Robin has to get up quickly before losing sight of her. She leaps across two large boulders to the other side of the stream and follows.
The girl calls through the trees. "Come on! No time to wait."
They run through the wood, past moss-covered tree trunks and out of the shade into a clearing. In the glare of the sun Robin loses sight of her. Where has she gone? Robin stops, just for a second, standing amongst foxgloves, pink and purple in the dazzling light.

In the shade, where coiled leaves of young ferns cling to the cliff face, Robin catches sight of a foot as the girl disappears behind a large boulder. There's a gap between the boulder and the cliff. Robin can only just squeeze through. Half way in, on the cliff side of the gap is a small tunnel. Robin crawls through. Wet knees and peaty hands; and there is the girl, crouching on the narrow edge of a perfect pool. Rock faces tower above the pool all around, forming a circle of sky overhead.

The girl turns towards Robin, finger to her lips and beckons with her arm for Robin to join her. Her eyes gleaming with excitement as she points to the centre of the pool. There's something about the dark water. Robin instinctively knows that it's very deep, "bottomless". In the centre bubbles appear and send giant blue and green dragonflies nervously into the air. Rippling rings spread out from the centre and then larger ripples.

Suddenly with all the power of a geezer, a huge golden carp leaps from the pool. It hangs, suspended momentarily. Instead of dropping back, it changes from gold to green and into human form, created by continuous, falling droplets. Then it speaks as though announcing itself to the world.

"I am the Water of Life.
Contained within all living forms.
Life emerged from me.
I water the crops that feed and nourish you.
Sustaining you in your blood and every cell of your body.
Everywhere that I touch becomes tree filled and full of flowers,
And when you enter my enfolding arms,
I take away everything that is unclean.
Love flows to you like rain kissing the earth,
And when you love, you are like water in a dry place."

There is a long pause; and a great stillness. A low mist gathers across the surface of the pool; wisps drawing towards the centre, joining and rising, to swirl upwards and onwards.

"This is the lifegiving cycle of water's transformation,
From ice to liquid to vapour.
Water rising gathers as cloud, reaches the heights and freezes,
To fall and begin the cycle again:

The same water cycling through time.
Uniting all.
As I pass through, I resonate with each form,
And carry that memory within me.
Holding the memory of the whole world's story,
In tears of sorrow and joy,
Records of the ancient past frozen in deep ice."

There is silence again, with just the sound of water dripping.

"Learn from water; ever flowing; ever transforming.
Fill your life from the depths to the brim,
And welcome transformation."

The mists clear and Robin looks again upon the wondrous liquid form.
"Act well.
Think wholesome thoughts.
Drink pure water and bathe your body with my blessing,
And renew yourself.

Remember me with these words.

Angel of Water.
Enter my blood,
And give the Water of Life to my whole body."

Everything around them holds its breath as two gulls call overhead. A few large snowflakes fall gently upon Robins' upturned face. Then time moves on again and all the drops of water fall at once back into the pool and the small girl has gone too. Robin crouches at the water's edge and catches a glimpse, for just a moment of a small frog following the tail of the giant, golden carp as it spirals out of sight: Back into the dark depths of the pool.
 She lies down, resting her face on one hand and trailing the other hand in the water, listening to the sound of the last of the ripples as they come lapping gently to shore and the water settled into deep, stillness.

A Handful of Seeds

Betty Fry has invited Robin for lunch with Bobby and the other boys and to meet Chris and Tsering. The two newest arrivals. Robin likes going to Betty's. It's noisy, boisterous and full of kindness; and food that her mum doesn't usually approve of but doesn't mind now and then, like white bread and chips; cakes and chocolate biscuits and VR games; and Bobby is the only one Robin can talk to about her encounters with the Angels and her crystal.

Robin meets Bobby and Tom, a younger boy, in the garden when she arrives and they're full of the morning's excitement. Two support workers; Stan and Ted had taken them out bird watching. They spent time in a hide looking through binoculars and then they were taken on a trip in a flat-bottomed boat, through a maze of reed beds and water channels. After that they met a man with a Falcon and a Barn Owl, fed them raw meat and watched them fly.

The only one not excited is Aaron. Robin passes him in the sitting room, slumped on the sofa, legs stretched out and shoulders hunched, reading a car magazine with an almost visible, black cloud over his head.

Robin goes on through to the kitchen and Betty smiles hello to her as she comes through the open door.

Larry's excited to see her. "Robin!"

"Hello Larry. What's the matter with Aaron, Betty?"

"Oh, he didn't go with the others. He thought Stan and Ted were just boring old men and didn't want to go. He's always the one who thinks that nothing good will come of things. He's like the man in the bible who thought he was looking at a handful of stones when he'd been given a handful of seeds. I'm trying to show him that it's worth giving things a chance. You don't always have to think the worst. Sometimes he misses out because of it."

There's a sudden wail from the other end of the table. Larry's only four and quite insecure, so spends most of his time close to Betty. He's mad about knights in shining armour and Betty has made him a shield out of cardboard that he's busily painting; only he's just spilt the green paint over it and is screaming. "Oh no! It's ruined. I've ruined it now."

Betty mops up the paint and has a look at it. "It's all right Larry. Look, you're just seeing spilled paint but look at this. I bet if you put an eye here; and some teeth here; and some claws here; maybe some red for flames, it will look just like a dragon. You see it wasn't that bad after all." Betty looks up at Robin and gives her a knowing wink.

Robin helps Betty lay the table and they send Larry off to find the other boys. Aaron's still in a bit of a mood and the new boy, Chris seems pretty low too. Bobby's trying to cheer him up but Robin can see that he's going to have trouble fitting in. The other new boy, Tsering, arrived a few days before and comes from Tibet. He had travelled via Nepal to India and then to England with his father, but had been taken away from his dad when they got to London. He's very small for his age but in other ways he seems older.

Robin feels quite shy about saying hello to him but she plucks up the courage. "Hello, I'm Robin."

Tsering's feeling shy too, but he smiles such a smile at her before retreating into what's on his plate, Robin's sure she's going to like him.

Chapter 5

Robin's in Trouble

On her way home, after visiting the boys, Robin takes her time picking flowers and looking for interesting bits of wood, for small sculptures that she makes from pieces that she picks up on her walks. She's looking out for dead ivy wrapped around twigs.

When Robin's nearly home, she cuts through the paddock and Polly follows by her side, up to the short cut over the fence into a vegetable field where Pete is planting out leeks.

"Oh, you're in trouble girl from what I can make out. Better hurry along and find out what it's all about."

Robin can't think why she would be in trouble. When she gets to the house her dad's car is in the driveway. As she opens the door, she can hear raised voices. Her heart starts beating too fast. She has to make herself go in.

"There you are. Where have you been?" Dad's obviously very cross. He's standing with a letter in his hand.

Mum's standing, leaning back against the Aga, looking down at her feet. It's a letter from Social Services. It's all because of something that happened the other weekend.

They often have people called WWOOFers. They come for free board and food, in return for helping out with the work on the land. On that weekend one of them was a nurse in her fifties, she was very fussy and complained about everything. She had caught Robin down by the beehives and Robin couldn't really understand why she'd made such a fuss about it.

Robin had been conducting an experiment. She'd read that bees do a waggle dance to tell other bees where to go and wanted to see it for herself. She spent a long time thinking about it and came up with a plan to put a jar with some honey in it on a wall and wait for the first bee. When the bee arrived, she would spray it with pink food dye. The plan was to follow it back to the hive to see if it did a dance and if other bees went straight to the jar afterwards, but it wasn't that easy. The bee stayed in the jar for ages. It got rather upset when she sprayed it. When it finally flew off, Robin was only able to follow it to three flowers before she lost track of it.

She decided to go to the hives and look for it there. This was when the nurse saw her. She was jumping up and down hysterically waiving her arms and calling, so Robin thought she'd better go and see what the matter was.

When Robin got to her, the nurse, (Robin couldn't remember her name) just grabbed her arm "Come with me." And hauled her to where her mother was working.

"What's the matter with you people? Don't you have any kind of safety procedures? I found this child down by the beehives, nothing to protect her, nothing to keep her out. I've a mind to report you to Social Services as irresponsible parents. It's bad enough that you let her just roam about on her own and I hear that she doesn't even go to school."

Mum told Robin to go and find something to do while they talked, so Robin didn't know what else had been said. She thought it had all been sorted out. Obviously not!

Her dad turns to her mum. "This is your fault too you know."

Her mum believes Robin is safe near bees, for as long as she has no fear, but her dad isn't so sure.

"That's not fair Dad. Mum knows the bees wouldn't hurt me."

"You see," continues her dad. "That's just what I mean."

Robin's mum isn't really afraid of the bees either. She wears all the protective clothing when she works with them, but the gloves are heavy and awkward and so she sometimes takes them off, without thinking much about it. The bees have never stung her and she knows she can trust Robin not to do anything silly around them, to annoy them, or to disturb the hives.

Her dad still seems unusually cross. He continues. "You just let her go on living in this fantasy world. You're getting too old for it Robin. And you need to respect that bees can be dangerous."

Robin can feel herself shaking. It makes her voice wobbly, which she hates. "I don't live in a fantasy world. It's real. I know it's all real and I do respect the bees, they know I do and stop shouting at Mum, it's not her fault, it's that silly nurse." Robin can't help herself. Whenever there's shouting, she just has to get away so she's already on her way out as she says this. She runs up the track towards the paddock.

Even though her dad knows nothing about her Angels, his words, "You live in a fantasy world." really heart her.

"It's real. I know it's real. I know it's all real."

When she gets to Polly in the paddock, she's so out of breath that she clings to her for a while until she can breathe again. Polly's body is warm and strong and comforting. Somehow the comfort of her allows Robins' feelings to rise up stronger and she begins to cry inconsolably. Then she just has to keep running. She runs on through the woods, beside the stream until she comes to a point where she can go no further, unless she climbs. There's a waterfall where people sometimes stop for picnics.

Angel of Wisdom.

Robin collapses down onto the grass across from the waterfall, hugging her knees and trying to control the sobs that just keep coming. There are so many things going around in her head. In her mind she can hear an echo of the mums in the kitchen laughing at her, and Deborah saying "That's just Squinty." She pictures going to school with all the noise of the children around her shouting and laughing at her, then Dad's words "You just let her go on living in a fantasy world." She hadn't known before that that was what he thought of her; and how seeing her dad at the party only made her miss him more and how much she loves him and how much she hates him for shouting at them!

"Why are you worrying so, little one?"
The voice is a mixture of laughter and such tender kindness. Robin stands up to see where it came from. She's sure there was no one there when she arrived and the only path in, is not far from where she's sitting.
She looks all around, then turns back towards the waterfall. A graceful, oriental woman in long robes, steps from a shallow alcove just to the side of the waterfall. An emerald green light, drapes of the aurora borealis, surrounding her. Accentuating the green of the mossy alcove and illuminating all that is close to her.
She hangs inches above the water momentarily and then in the blink of an eye she's standing in front of Robin, holding out the flower of a wild rose.

"Your troubles are like this rose.
Hold it close to your face, you only see the rose.

Place it further away and it becomes small and unimportant.
Souls are born into this world to learn lessons through feeling.
A special world of feeling.
Pain is a necessary part of the lesson
This world of feeling has to teach.
Learn to let go of the self-pity that distracts from the truth.
The truth that you have come into this life to experience."

She changes position in an instant and is sitting on a nearby rock, clasping the ankle that is crossed over the opposite knee and leaning forward towards Robin.

Robin sits back down on the grass to listen.

"You are suffering.
It is part of life's journey,
Until all are free of suffering.
If you feel misunderstood.
It is up to you to help people to understand.
Suffering comes from hopelessness.
But you can create hope through action.
Action out in the world and action in your mind.
You can choose those thoughts,
That bring hope and understanding."

Robin can't usually look into anyone's eyes for long but now she can't turn away from the kindness in the woman's gaze. The longer they look the broader their smiles become, but at the same time she realises that the woman is gradually fading. And then she is gone, leaving Robin alone, with only the sound of the waterfall.

She stands to leave and there is a hoot from an owl as it glides over Robin's head and a sudden tap on her shoulder. Robin nearly jumps out of her skin. She spins round to see an old lady wearing a cloak of owl feathers and with no pause and no introduction she speaks.

"Wisdom brings the gift of truth to the troubled mind.
Your mind is like a garden.
You can choose to plant and nurture the thoughts that nourish you
And you can weed out the thoughts that shade out the light.
Reconnect to that greater power that is behind all things.
And seek Wisdom for the answers.

The most powerful healer is the Wise Word.
We create Heaven in life,
Through good thoughts, good words and good deeds.
These are the precious gifts of Wisdom.
Wisdom makes us free from fear,
Wide of heart
And easy in conscience.

Summon the Angel of Wisdom with me now."

She steps forward and clasps a surprisingly strong, bony hand over Robin's forehead while speaking the words.
"Repeat these words after me

Angel of Wisdom,
Descend upon my Thinking Body,
And enlighten all my thoughts."

Robin repeats the words, "Angel of Wisdom. Descend upon my Thinking Body and enlighten all my thoughts."
She stands with her eyes closed, transfixed in the old woman's grasp and then she feels. Freedom. There are tears again but this time tears of deep relief. The idea that she can choose what to think seems so simple and obvious but is something Robin has never thought about before: That she can choose to let go of thoughts that make her unhappy and can choose instead to concentrate on solutions that bring peace of mind and hope; it gives her an enthusiasm to look at her problems in a new light. She gradually becomes aware once more of the sound of the water falling and opens her eyes and finds herself alone again.
Robin undresses and wades through the shallow water into the pool created by the waterfall. She breaks through the curtain of water with her hand, feeling its power pushing down against her palm. Then she steps into the full icy force of it. She lifts her face upwards, the water pounding down onto her forehead and she remembers the words of the Angel of Water. "Act well. Think wholesome thoughts. Drink pure water and bathe your body with my blessing and renew yourself."
When she steps out again her mind feels refreshed and clear.

Dad

Robin is apprehensive about heading home but she starts off down the track and turns a corner and there's her dad on his way up. He stands and waits for her and when she catches up with him, he puts his arm around her. They walk that way in silence for a short while but the path is too narrow, so they have to separate.

Robin walks behind him, not knowing what to say to him. The truth is Robin's ashamed of running away whenever there's shouting. She feels it means that she's a coward at heart, when she likes to think of herself as brave and daring. Especially when she joins in with the boys at Betty's, doing dares to show off. She doesn't like thinking of herself as someone who runs away so easily and she doesn't like her dad seeing her as someone like that either. She's happy to spend more time remembering what was said to her at the waterfall, and Dad seems lost in his own thoughts too.

They're half way down, where the track becomes wider and flatter, walking side by side again, when he finally speaks. "I don't really think you're living in a fantasy world Robin. The truth is that's what I've been thinking about myself recently. I've been thinking that this life we've brought you into was my fantasy and I haven't managed to make it work.

"I've messed things up with your mum too, and I'm worried that I brought you up without preparing you for the rest of the world that's out there. Now everything's changing for you because I can't make my fantasy work and I'm concerned about you. I know you don't want to go to that school. I was already worried before that letter from Social Services and then it just seemed to confirm how irresponsible we've been with you. I was angry with myself really, not with you and Mum."

Robin walks on without answering for a while. She's holding the crystal in her pocket, calling on the Angel of Wisdom to help her say something that will give Dad peace of mind. Then it just comes to her.

"You haven't failed me Dad. There are so many things I have that some children will never have. I know how to grow and cook healthy food; and I know so much about nature and I've learnt so much from looking after the animals. Like you can't not feed them or muck them out just because you don't feel like it.

And it doesn't do any good getting impatient or bad tempered with them, just because they don't do what you want; and I love to work hard. Surely, they're things I'll always need in life? And I'm strong and healthy and I'm not behind with my school work; and recently I learnt that you can't expect life not to change. It's like a river with all its twists and turns and you have to swim with it; and now you're staying in London so much, maybe I can come and stay with you sometimes and go to museums and concerts and things; and learn even more."

Robin's dad's thinking how much she's grown up this year. "Well, we must have got something right Robin, those are certainly wise words. Thank you. It puts my mind at ease to know that that's how you feel."

Her words have made Robin feel better too. It's the first time she's tried this more positive way of looking at things and so they finish their walk home across the paddock together, hand in hand.

High overhead, two small stars wink at them, in a gold and rose-pink sunset.

Chapter 6

Social Services

Wednesday, the day arranged for the social worker's visit. Robin's dad has put up a fence with a gate in it, across the corner of the field where the beehives are, with a sign saying "Caution Bees". Actually, it's worked out rather well, because Mum can plant a couple of fruit trees in there in the autumn, without worrying about protecting them from the goats.

Robin's standing at the kitchen sink doing the washing up while looking out of the kitchen window. She remembers standing on a chair in the same spot when she was little, doing the washing up with Mum. She used to like putting washing up liquid in the tea pot and filling it with water until all the suds came spewing out of the spout; or she'd press the Pyrex baking dish into the water and look through the bottom of it at the secret world of cutlery, in the grey water, under the surface layer of bubbles.

They're all rather nervous about the visit without really knowing why. Robin's dad can't be there because of work so her mum's going to have to deal with Mr. Christian on her own. Finally, the doorbell rings. Robin had watched Mr. Christian open the yard gate and make his way to the door. She'd pictured someone stern, in a suit, carrying a briefcase. But he's not like that. Zac Christian's family originally came from Jamaica and he has lived in England all his life. Zac looks more like one of their friends, relaxed and cheerful.

Robin's mum opens the door and introduces herself but somehow from the moment he introduces himself, Zac's manor makes Robin feel that he's her guest.

"I just need to speak with your mother for a bit Robin and then I'd like you to show me around."

After he's spoken with her mum, Robin shows Zac the poly-tunnel and the gardens and the colourful array of chickens and geese they keep.

"Hasn't one escaped?" He points towards a large black and white speckled hen. She's enjoying a dust bath in the sun-scorched earth at the corner of the stable.

"Oh no, that's Daisy, she doesn't think she's a chicken. She was a chick I had to look after when Buster was a puppy. I think she thinks she's a dog. She'll even see Buster off his food and eat it herself, if the kitchen door's open when I feed him and she usually pecks at people's ankles if she doesn't like the look of them, so she must think you're alright. If we put her in with the other chickens, she pecks all their feathers out. She's awful but we love her."

Zac is impressed by how clean and well-looked after the animals are.

"That's my job," Robin says with pride. "Would you like to see the bees now?"

Robin leads Zac across the field to the beehives, chatting away about everything she knows about bees. He asks her what had happened on the day that the nurse complained.

She tells him all about her plan, to see the bee's dance. "…You see bees aren't out to get you the way some people think they are. They're far too busy. They only get agitated if you do something silly to threaten them and you just don't do that: Especially around the hives. Wasps. They can be much more spiteful. They're the ones you have to watch out for!"

Zac can see that the fence and sign are new, but that's all right. "Well everything looks pretty in order here. You know Robin; I shouldn't think I'll have you on my books for very long. I was mainly here to talk about your education, so you need to make use of me now if you have any problems. I'm here for you. I'm your Social Worker."

Robin's a bit worried by what he could mean. Could he be implying something? She can't think of anything he could possibly help her with and she knows that her dad doesn't like this intrusion by the authorities into their lives. "No. Everything's fine. I can't think of anything."

"What about school? Your mum tells me you're worried about that. Are you worried about being bullied?"

Robin is leaning over fishing about in her sandal for a stone that's caught there. She looks up into Zac's broad face and kind, watery brown eyes. "No, well yes. It's not nice. It's something I have to deal with. There are always some kids who call me Squinty, but I think Mum and Dad are more worried about that than I am. They don't really believe me when I say it's not that."

"What is it then? Is it the work?"

"No. It's hard to describe. It doesn't sound that important but, it's that, when I'm with a lot of children I can't cope with the noise. It sounds silly I know. Mum and Dad think it's something I'll just get used to but it really affects me. I can't focus on anything when there's a lot of noise around me. I end up in this kind of fuzzy bubble, with everything outside like an echo, and then I can't make out what people are saying to me because I can't shut out the noise. It gives me a terrible headache." The words just sort of tumble out. Robin can feel a lump in her throat and tears welling in her eyes. There's something about Zac that allows the full force of how she feels to rise up and make her heart ache.

"Well, I can see how serious this is for you Robin. I do have one or two ideas: Things that could be put in place to help you. I won't say what they are now until I'm sure. I'll look into some possibilities and get back to you as soon as I can."

Buster

Robin's feeling quite light headed. The social workers' visit had been nothing like she had feared. She had been worried that it was going to create problems, but it turned out that Zac was the one person who listened to her real problem seriously. He might even be able to help. She opens the porch door to reach for the dog lead and calls to her mother. "I'm taking Buster out. OK?"

Buster doesn't usually need a lead. Robin trained him not to chase other animals long ago. She'd only been allowed to have a puppy on the strict understanding that she would take him to puppy class and learn to train him herself. The first class was like a comedy show. The polished wooden floor of the village hall was like an ice rink for dogs. They were all told to trot round the hall in a circle together, with their puppies on leads, but the floor was so shiny, when each puppy took the corners, they slid in a wide sweep, their feet splaying out on ungainly puppy legs as they glided round and collided in a tangle of leads with the puppy in front. Teaching them to fetch, ended up with the owners as disobedient as the puppies, as they skimmed toys across the floor to see whose puppy could do the longest slide. Even the adults!

They were given some very stern homework that Robin took on full heartedly, and the following week the trainer said Robin must have a natural talent for dog training.

Robin decides to take the dog lead because she wants to take the short cut to the sandy beach. She doesn't normally do this because it means cutting across a field that belongs to people who don't like trespassers, so if she gets caught, she doesn't want to be accused of being irresponsible with the dog too. She just wants to get down to the beach as quickly as possible. They start off at a trot and when they get to the fallow field, she puts the lead on Buster and they run across it as fast as they can; Buster barging his way across the awkward ruts of dry earth panting with over excitement. Robin loves running with Buster. He keeps her going so that she can run much further than when she runs by herself, and when he's on the lead it feels like he tows her much faster than she can normally run.

They take the steep, sandy path down to the sea through bramble bushes and spiky grasses and the pale grey thistles that grow like holly in the sand. Robin's gasping for breath, relishing the fresh salty air as it fills her lungs.

They get to the bottom of the path and she sits on the sand with her back against a rock. She puts her crystal in an indent on the top of a rock beside her in the sun. Still catching her breath, with each outward breath some part of herself settles back into her body, like the different layers of a Russian doll. The worry over the last weeks about the changes in their lives and the social worker's visit, had left her in pieces and now with each outward breath she's becoming whole and connected to the earth again and each breath in, feels full of clarity and hope. She sits watching Buster. He's playing at the edge of the waves with a piece of driftwood covered in seaweed. He's already been in the water and his short fur is clinging to his body, exposing his barrel chest and pink tummy and his legs are covered in sand.

Angel of Air

Robin picks up the crystal and her sandals and walks bare foot, down the beach towards Buster. Every now and then she stops to look around. The wind comes in gusts and with each gust she's sure she can hear children and sometimes feint, tinkling sounds.

Robin looks back at Buster. He's sitting looking at something beyond her. His head tilted with a quizzical frown and ears pricked forward. She looks behind her and sees something coming towards them across the sands: A small whirlwind or "dust devil." As it gets closer there are more all around her and from each comes the sound of children's laughter and wind chimes, getting louder and then fainter, as they move near her and away again. They're dancing a dance all around her. Robin feels compelled to join in with them in wild, joyous, abandon. Dancing and swirling, turning and turning with arms outstretched, laughing across the wet sands and skipping through wavelets at the water's edge. Until she's so dizzy and breathless that she ends up on her back on the warm sand, laughing up at the sky as it turns circles overhead.

Buster's trying to get her attention. He had joined in the dancing with her, gleefully chasing small whirlwinds in circles, stopping to bark at them and then chasing after them again. Now he's urgently licking her face and nudging her with his nose. He barks at her a couple of times then licks her face again. The little whirlwinds are joining together. There's a sound as if all the surrounding air is being sucked in with them and as they became one large whirlwind a young man appears, suspended in the centre. He's dressed in loose white trousers and has sky blue skin. His hair is white and there are wings on his feet.

Robin sits up, leaning back, resting her weight on her out stretched arms behind her, her face turned up towards him in wonder.

"I am the Herald of the Angel of Air.
The Air that spreads the perfume of sweet-smelling fields,
And the sweet grasses after rain.
The wind that carries seeds and insects,
To bring new life to new lands across the seas.
The Air that carries water as it cycles the Earth,
And that unites all in the sweetness of breath."

He's suspended within swirling winds, zigzagging in front of her, just to stay in one place.

> "The sky-blue sphere that surrounds and protects you,
> Sustaining the Earth within it.
> Regenerated and purified,
> Through the Earthly Mother's great lungs of forest and field and sea.
> The catalyst to all bodily functions and the Soul's vitality.
> The Air that lifts the wings of all that fly."

With his words the winds spiralling around him become the wings of many birds. The sound of the wind turns into the sound of many wings as they circle once more around him, then fly off in a unified cloud, rippling into the distance.

He had seemed incapable of staying still but now he's sitting at rest beside her and continues to speak. "The Earth breaths and you breath with her. Your body is sustained by air for its' survival but there's more to air than molecules and just as your Soul is essential to you and invisible, so too is the vitality or "prana" carried in the air. It grants not only life but also the "Life Force" to your whole being.

"Breathe deep through your nose and draw in all the layers of the air's vitality. Take the breath deep into your belly until your lungs are full to the top; Hold it, and savour it as it penetrates your blood and then let it out through the mouth, from the bottom of your lungs, to rest for a while, relaxed and complete before the next new breath begins.

"Close your eyes and breathe now Robin and know each new breath is a new beginning.

"Breathe deep and speak these words whenever you wish to summon the air's vitality.

> *Angel of the Air,*
> *Enter my lungs and grant the Air of Life to my whole body."*

Robin sits with her eyes closed, breathing deep to the rhythm of the waves. Feeling the vitality in the air. The Sun is warm on her face and around her the world is at peace.

Deborah's Secret

Robin opens her eyes; the tide is going out. Buster has been sitting beside her for a while and she decides to leave him off the lead and walk around the point to the next beach, taking a longer way home.

She has to climb over large rocks to get around the point, working out which routes aren't going to lead to dead ends and stopping now and then, to examine life in the rock pools.

When the rocks finally turn her towards the next beach, she can see someone sitting on a breakwater in the distance, at the other end of the beach. She ambles along the ribbon of sand, parallel to the sea, a few strides from the water's edge, where the waves always leave behind seaweed and shells and other odd pieces of treasure. She enjoys picking her way through this, occasionally looking at something more closely and then putting it down again or throwing a stick into the waves for Buster.

The next time she looks up she's close enough to make out that it's Deborah sitting on some rocks ahead of her. Robin can see that she's sitting with her head in her hands and seems to be upset. Robin jogs towards her calling to her but she doesn't respond. It's only when Robin gets close enough to Deborah to rest her hand on Deborah's wrist that she finally looks up. Her eyes and cheeks are red from crying but something else is wrong.

Deborah's holding a hand to her throat and panting, she only just manages to get the words out. "I can't breathe, Robin."

Robin doesn't know it but Deborah's having a panic attack. She knows she's going to have to help Deborah somehow because even if she phoned someone it would take them too long to get there and any way, she knows there's no signal down on the beach.

She uses the calming voice that she uses on animals when they're afraid. "It's OK Deborah. It's going to be alright." Robin sits down beside Deborah and puts her hand over Deborah's diaphragm. "Just breathe with me Deborah. Nice and slow. In…and out… Breathe down into my hand. In…and out… Breathe in through your nose and out through your mouth, deep and slow."

Deborah's breathing gradually calms down into the same rhythm as Robin's. Then Deborah puts her arm around Robin's shoulders and they sit leaning against one another, looking out across the sea. Robin can't believe how easily they feel like the best of friends.

Sitting side by side with their heads touching and their hearts joined.

"Thanks' Robin. I feel like such an idiot."

"You don't have to be sorry. What happened?"

"It's my mum. I know your dad and my dad are friends but your parents don't really know my mum. Not many people know about it but she has such a bad temper. When she shouts at me, it feels like a hole has been ripped in my insides. We had such a row today. She really scared me. We were in the car and I told her I didn't want to go to dancing lessons any more. We were arguing about it and she just slammed on the brakes to have a go at me. She didn't even look to see if any cars were behind us. A van driver went screeching past us with his hand on the horn and we skidded for a bit before we stopped. We were both shaking.

"When we got home, she kept going on at me about how it was my fault. Look what I made her do; that sort of thing. I could feel her seething all morning. I hate that feeling. Tiptoeing around, waiting for the next explosion. And then it came. We were in the kitchen and she was on the phone to some insurance people; she'd lost a piece of paper that she said had been on the table and accused me of moving it. She just went ballistic and threw a cup that broke on the kitchen floor. Yelling at me to get out of her sight. She said it was all my fault that she had to give up dancing and how ungrateful I was for all the money they'd spent on my dancing classes. Dad told me a while ago that she'd tried to get jobs as a dancer for a couple of years before he met her and it hadn't worked out. He said she seemed happy to marry him and have a different life.

"So now you know my secret. We're not the perfect family we try to make out to be."

Robin had begun to see that there was something making Deborah unhappy but she'd never guessed that Deborah had such a hard time at home. It made her own reaction to merely raised voices, seem rather pathetic. "What are you going to do now?"

Deborah sits staring out across the sea for a while longer and then lets out a heavy sigh. "I suppose I should be getting home now. Dad will be back and anyway, after Mum's been angry, for her it's as though nothing much has happened and she can't understand why anyone should be upset. I'll just go up to my room as usual. Any way I need to pack a bag. We're going back to London tomorrow morning. I wanted to stay here for the whole half term, but they want to go back for a business dinner. Then come back.

"Why don't you come and stay with me? Do you think your parents would let you?"

If someone had told Robin yesterday that she was going to invite Deborah to stay the night, she would have thought they were mad so she hopes she's doing the right thing.

"I don't think they'll mind, Mum's usually quite glad if she can get someone else to look after me. I'm going to boarding school after the summer. I'm looking forward to it. I think we'll both be a lot happier."

They agree that Robin will get her mum to phone and arrange it. Robin walks with Deborah the short distance to her cottage. She always feels scruffy next to Deborah. She's the kind of person who always looks like she's wearing brand new clothes, from expensive London shops. She's taller than Robin and very beautiful, with immaculate straight black hair. Robin's thinking to herself that Deborah's not going to look like that for long if she stays with them and then she starts worrying that Deborah might end up hating it. After all, Robin's still going to have to do all her chores and Deborah will just have to muck in.

Chapter 7

Polly

Deborah arrives, with "Hunter" wellies and a stylish suitcase; just as Robin's filling a bucket of water for Polly.

When Robin's mum has finished talking with Deborah's mum, she comes over to them.

"Why don't you girls take Polly to the paddock and I'll get one of the WWOOFers to do the mucking out. Then you can feed the chickens and collect the eggs."

Deborah turns to Robin, puzzled. "What are WWOOFers?"

"World Wide Opportunities on Organic Farms. It's a way that people who like to work on the land can come and help us out for free meals and camping. We've got six at the moment. They're camping here for a few days. Actually, they've invited us for supper at their camp tonight which is a treat as we usually have to cook for them."

Polly's misbehaving. It's unusual for her. She's fidgeting backwards and forwards: Hooves ringing on concrete. Tugging at Robin's arm, chewing on her bit and rolling her eyes.

Robin gives her a few reassuring pats. "Calm down Polly." Deborah has been gradually backing away.

"Are you scared of her Deborah? That's what's wrong with her then. Sorry, I didn't think, you need to be properly introduced. Horses are very sensitive to body language; she's picking up on your nerves. I can show you how to calm her down if you like."

Deborah's not sure. She doesn't like horses. Some of her school friends are besotted with them but Deborah feels they have anxious, unreadable eyes that she can't really trust. "I'm not sure. She doesn't like me now, does she?"

"That's easily fixed. Honest. Why don't you just give it a try?"

Deborah gives in, reluctantly. "OK then, I'll give it a go, as long as you promise to stay close by."

"Of course, I will. Now, the first thing you need to do is relax. Just stand with your eyes closed for a minute and make your breathing calm and quiet."

While Deborah has her eyes closed, Robin loosens her hold on Polly's rains so that Polly won't feel any tension through them. "You can open your eyes now. Just stay relaxed with your breathing quiet and don't look at her. Just move slowly towards her sideways on, so that she doesn't feel threatened and keep your breathing calm. She likes it if you say a few words to her or just say her name a few times."

Deborah concentrates on keeping her breathing calm and does everything just as Robin says and Robin can sense that Polly is already more relaxed.

"She's OK now, you can stroke her neck if you like."

Deborah strokes Polly's neck for a short while. "There's a good girl Polly."

Polly turns her head and rubs her face affectionately against Deborah. The weight of Polly's head almost pushing her off-balance.

"That wasn't hard was it?" Robin says, giggling a little. "Here, give her this bit of carrot. Just give it to her with your hand flat."

Deborah thinks she'll never forget that moment when Polly turned her head and nuzzled up against her. The fact that it was done through Polly's free will touched Deborah in a way that she hadn't expected from an animal before. She will never again think of animals as alien to her in quite the way that she had in the past.

Robin leads Polly through the gate and then holds out the rains for Deborah. "Here you are. You can lead her the rest of the way."

Deborah takes the rains and feels proud of how beautiful Polly is, as though she's her own. She leads Polly to the paddock and it gives her an unexpected thrill when some walkers turn to watch them.

Friendship

Robin's surprised when she finds that Deborah is actually a hard worker. She doesn't like the chickens much and doesn't want to try holding one when Robin shows her how. But she enjoys feeding them and collecting the eggs. Then they clean up the tack room, where all the horse paraphernalia is stored.

When they join the WWOOFers after lunch, they work in the vegetable patches, weeding and planting; and pushing wheelbarrows, feeding a bonfire and the compost heap.

Deborah seems to really enjoy mucking in with every one and still somehow manages to keep herself immaculate by the end of the day.

It's getting close to supper time and they make their way to the WWOOFers' camp, to help prepare the food: They're having a big stew of vegetables and dumplings made with fresh herbs, to go with bread and cheese. Deborah enjoys the relaxed feeling between everyone as they wash and chop vegetables together. Anile, a German girl, shows her how to make salad, adding dandelion leaves, wild garlic, nasturtium and borage flowers.

When they've finished, they sit down on logs around the camp fire, drinking fresh camomile tea while they watch supper cook in a large pot, hung on a tripod over the flames. Deborah's sitting beside Anile. She looks as if she's in her early twenties, dressed in shorts with her knees tucked up into a large, fluffy, polar neck sweater, keeping her long legs warm against the now chilly night air.

Deborah's sitting among these friends, feeling a bond with them, created by the afternoon's work together; she enjoyed the playful, cooperative atmosphere they shared when preparing the evening meal together. Sitting around the fire with them, she listens to their good-natured banter, not contributing but not feeling left out either. She experiences a sensation in her heart and throat, an overwhelming happiness at sharing this inclusion: A sense of family and warmth that she hasn't experienced before. She looks across the fire at Robin and Robin looks up at the same time and their eyes meet in glowing, simple happiness. Robin's peering at some cards laid out on the ground at Brian's feet.

"What are you looking at Robin?"

"Come over and see. They're animal cards."

Deborah joins them, looking at the beautifully drawn animals on the cards.

Brian's explaining to Robin. "They come from the American Indian tradition. There are a lot more but I only use the cards with animals we find here in the U.K. You can use them in different ways. You can just have a question in your mind and pick one card to help you with the answer; or you can lay them out in a particular pattern and that can be read to tell you things about the direction your life is going in; or you may have met an animal in your life and want to find out what it's message might have been. When you have enough experience and knowledge of the cards you can usually tell which animals different people are."

"What animal do you think I am?"

"Oh you're definitely a crow."

Robin's not very pleased by this. She doesn't really like the idea of being a crow.

"Don't look so disappointed Robin. Crows are magic. The story goes that Crow was fascinated by her own shadow and she kept pecking at it until it woke up and ate her. The shadow world is the world of magic behind everything. So she sees the laws behind everything, not just laws we invent for ourselves, but the hidden world of magic behind this world. Crow people are often in touch with magic, but they have trouble expressing their secret self. It's important that Crow people learn to express their own truth. The Mayans think of crow as cross-eyed, looking through first one eye and then the other. They say that this gives Crow the ability to see into the future. So you see Robin, Crow's not such a bad animal to be."

She does feel better knowing this about crow. It helps her make sense of the feeling she often has, that she can't put into words the truth that she can see in her thinking.

"What animal do you think I am?" asks Deborah.

"I think you're a butterfly. Butterflies aren't only beautiful; they are the masters of self-transformation and know the importance of taking time to complete each stage. So you have the egg stage, the caterpillar stage, the chrysalis stage and finally the butterfly. Each stage as crucial to transformation as the other."

Robin can see this about Deborah too. Something in the way she finished clearing up the cleaning things in the tack room. A natural instinct to leave the job completed. She had rinsed out the wash cloths and hung them over the edge of the large, stone basin, with such peaceful concentration. Robin would have just squeezed them out and chucked them back into the bucket. There was something accomplished about even the smallest thing Deborah did.

"Have you had any encounters with animals lately Robin?"

"Well a little while ago I saw a raven."

"Raven is to do with magic too. The Indians believe that if you see a raven it may be telling you that you're about to have an experience that teaches you about life's magic, an awakening. It's the power of the unknown at work, something special is about to happen."

The conversation ends as Frank strikes a chord on the guitar and starts singing in a low voice, accompanied by Jo on the violin, her notes drifting into the night, now gathering around them. Stars bright overhead.

From where she's sitting Deborah can just make out the sea in one direction, the blue of the horizon still lighter than the dark of the sky overhead. In the other direction she can see the friendly lights from the windows of the house a field away, tucked in against the solid blackness of the woods. She feels so at ease here in a world that's so different from her own.

Frank has put the stew pot back over the fire, full of water for the washing up and when his song ends, she and Robin offer to help. Deborah has never washed up like this before. She's kneeling over a washing up bowl, trying to see by the light of a large torch but it always seems to cast shadows just where she's looking, with the odd blade of grass floating on the surface of the water. "I've never been camping," she says. "I didn't know it could be such fun. Mum won't go anywhere without an en-suite bathroom."

"We don't have to go back to the house." Answers Robin. "We can get my tent and a couple of sleeping bags and sleep here if you like. The tent's easy to put up. It's one of those pop-up ones. As long as you promise to help me collapse it down again in the morning!"

They walk back to the house together and gather up what's needed and in no time are happily tucked up in sleeping bags; with the front of the tent open, showing a glimpse of the flickering fire and the night sky. Somehow the murmur of lowered voices from a couple of people still sitting by the fire accentuates the quietness all around them.

Deborah surprises Robin saying, "I'm sorry I've been mean to you before Robin. I don't know why I do that. You've been a good friend to me and Bobby has too. I just don't know how to be with him. Sometimes he's like a baby and sometimes he's like a grown up and sometimes he seems to know how I'm feeling, like he can read my mind. Once he gave me a hug and I just started crying. I thought I was fine before that. It spooked me."

Robin knows what she means. She's had hugs like that from him.

Deborah continues, "And he's too affectionate for me. I'm not used to that. It makes me feel awkward. Anyway, today's been such a special day for me. I really hope we can be friends."

They talk on into the night, getting to know each other for the first time in the months that they've been put together by their parents. Deborah falls asleep first but Robin takes a little longer, holding the crystal on her chest, feeling it amplify her heart with gladness as she thinks about how different Deborah is when she's with these warm hearted, open people; and how wrong she'd been with her first judgements of Deborah; and what sort of life she has; and how good it makes her feel to see Deborah happy.

As Robin drifts towards sleep the crystal speaks into her heart.

"Love shall flow as a fountain
From one to another
And as it is spent so shall it be replenished."

Chapter 8

Tsering

Robin is on her way to Betty's to say goodbye to Chris. He hasn't been with Betty for long, but she has got to know him in that short time. His mum's coming out of hospital and Robin knows he's looking forward to going home.

The house is one of a row of houses, cut into the hillside, overlooking the sea. As she climbs the three flights of steps that lead from the road up to the front gate, she can hear Chris practicing the piano. He's brilliant, even on Betty's croncky old upright. Robin's mum often listens to Classic FM when she's in the house and the other day, while she was mopping the conservatory floor, Robin heard on the radio, one of the pieces that Chris practices. For the couple of weeks that he'd been there, Chris has taken the early morning train to London each Saturday, for lessons with a teacher at one of the big music colleges.

As Robin opens the garden gate, she can see Tsering sitting on the front doorstep in the warm sunshine. Betty has given him a bowl of soapy water and he's busily washing some small treasures that he'd brought with him from Tibet; laying them out to dry on the piece of Tibetan material that they'd been wrapped in. Robin joins him on the step as he holds up for her to see, the small brass bell that he's just finished scrubbing. Already drying on the cloth are a tiny lion or dog, carved out of green stone and three Tibetan coins. Robin waits to see what will be drawn through the curtain of soapsuds next. It's a hand length statue, carved out of some hard, dark wood.

Chris has finished practicing the piano and joins them. Squatting behind them, he peers over their shoulders. "That's a Quan Yin isn't it?" he asks. "Mum has one in her bedroom."

"Yes. Well, she's Green Tara in my country and Quan Yin in China. My dad bought her for me. Actually, this one is a Chinese Quan Yin. My dad didn't realise the difference. He bought it because Mum was devoted to Green Tara and he said that she would help Mum watch over me. I don't mind that he got it wrong. It reminds me that the Chinese aren't so different from us after all."

Robin has been sitting silent, entranced. It's very like the Eastern Maiden that she'd seen at the waterfall. The statue's even sitting in the same way. One foot crossed over the top of the other knee. Robin has never doubted that her visions are real, but she hasn't told anyone about them, except Bobby, because she didn't think they were a part of life for most people. And now here is her vision: Part of the normal world. How can it be? "But I've seen her."

"Yes, she's getting better known in your country now."

"No. I mean I've seen her for real. She spoke to me at the waterfall."

"Really? There have been lots of people in my country with stories about talking with her, but I didn't know she appeared in this country."

Tsering's surprised that someone from a Western culture would encounter Tara. Robin's surprised that Tsering sees it as quite normal to talk to such a being and that other people do too. Robin tells him about the Eastern maiden, how she'd spoken to Robin about suffering, about it being a part of life until all are free of suffering and that we can choose thoughts that bring peace of mind and hope. As he listens, Tsering sits very still with his eyes shut, so still that Robin and Chris are drawn into his stillness for a while after Robin has finished speaking.

Robin breaks the silence. "What can you tell us about her Tsering?"

Tsering's glad to have the chance to share his world. He feels very different and left out with these English children. The children he'd met before he arrived at Betty's hadn't been interested in where he came from.

He remembers sitting on a rock, on the outskirts of his village for the last time, waiting for Dad and the others. He was looking down on the plane below, where the Nomads were grazing yaks, the sound of a Tibetan flute could just be heard coming from their camp. The clear, blue skies and the mountains; so crisp in the thin air that they looked like they were made of steel, the dazzling light reflecting off snowy caps.

These English children knew nothing. Uncles in the recent past shot, or taken to prison by Chinese soldiers and your language, history and culture banned. How quickly he had to grow up to survive the dangerous journey across the freezing Himalayas and the Death Pass near the border with Nepal.

There was even a path that they took, where they had to try to ignore the frozen body of someone from a group before them, who hadn't made it.

No, these children could never know.

Tsering pauses for a moment looking at the beloved little statue that his dad had given him. He wonders if Robin can really understand Tara. "My mum told me that, in a way her form is created by all the different minds that believe in her. To us she is pure compassion. She is real, a Bodhisattva. She is beyond the cycles of being born and dyeing and born again. In an instant she could step into another existence but she's chosen, out of compassion, to stay. To help us until all of us reach what we call enlightenment. She's not really even a she or a he. That's just the way we experience her."

Robin thinks about what Tsering has said for a while and still wants to know more. "So you believe we're born over and over again?"

"Yes. Our spiritual leader, the Dalai Lama was a Lama in another life. When a Lama dies, we find him again by searching the villages for children who seem special and then test them. In one of the tests the monks show them objects that were important to the Lama before he died. They're mixed in with other objects and then they know which is the right child, because he recognises his past possessions."

Chris is listening too. "That's what Mum says about me. Every time I sit down at the piano, I feel like I'm just relearning it. Like I must have known how to play in another life; and my nan says that the first time I saw the piano at her house, when I was about three, I just sat down and started playing simple scales and tunes and she thought I'd been having lessons."

The phone had been ringing while they were talking. It stops and Betty calls for Chris. Robin turns and watches Chris go down the hall with an inexplicable feeling of apprehension for him. Betty shuts the door and Robin's still sitting beside Tsering as he lays the statue down on the Tibetan cloth.

"I'm sorry about your mum Tsering."

"That was when my dad came. I didn't know him before that. My uncle wrote to him because they couldn't afford to keep me after she died."

"Where had he been before that?"

"Dad's English. He had to leave Tibet before I was born.

Mum said he couldn't come into the country again but she made me learn English. She said I ought to be able to speak my father's language. He had to come in over the mountains illegally to get me and we had to leave the same way."

"Wasn't that really dangerous?"

"He's an experienced climber. When he arrived, he stayed for about a month while he and some village men organised how to take a group out with us to Nepal. It's still difficult for some people to get permission to leave the country. Somehow he managed to get my name put onto his British passport. He thought because I'm small we'd get away with saying I'm younger than I am so that I wouldn't need a separate passport."

"Weren't you scared of getting caught?"

"Yes, we got away with it going to India after Nepal but then we had to get on a plane from New Delhi to London. It was so strange. We were suddenly on a plane in this comfortable world, when we'd just come from people getting frostbite in the mountains, with not enough food and trying to get to sleep when it's so cold. Then we got to London and we were caught. Dad was smuggling hashish for money so he's in prison and I'm stuck waiting to have the right legal papers. They did a DNA test so they know he really is my dad."

"Don't worry Tsering. Betty will look after you. She's such a good-hearted person. Will your dad be in prison for long?"

"I don't know. He's still waiting for his trial. Anyway, I don't know if I'd ever want to live with him? He was my hero when we were in the mountains. I think some of us might have died if he hadn't been with us. There are dangerous mistakes you can make up there, but when we got down into the towns, I saw another side to him. He rushed everything and made bad decisions. It's like he has so many things going on in his head all the time and he can't be still, to think clearly and he got a bit paranoid. I think that's because he was doing something illegal so he was always afraid. I know he thought he was doing the right thing when he came to get me, but I wish he'd taken me to Dharamshala when we were in India. That's where most of the Tibetans go. I really want to be a Buddhist monk."

Robin can hear raised voices, and a door slams inside the house. "I'm just going to go and see if Chris is all right." She leaves Tsering, sitting alone again with his few treasures and his thoughts.

Unfulfilled Hopes

Robin enters the house to find Betty leaning with her back against the wall in the hallway, her arms folded and her eyes closed.

"Are you alright Betty?"

"I'm alright dear. It's Chris's mum. She's taken a turn for the worst and won't be coming out of hospital today after all. Chris is very upset. He was so hoping to go home with her today. He's gone off out. I think he'll need to have some time on his own for a bit."

Robin follows Betty into the kitchen. "Did you know Tsering was really hoping to become a monk? He says he's worried about living with his dad and wishes that he could have stayed in India with the other Tibetans."

"No, I didn't. I'm glad you told me. I know he's only known his dad for a few months. Well anything's possible. Let's go and have a look on the computer and see what we can find out."

Robin follows Betty into the study.

"You're better at this than I am Robin. What do you think we should search for first?"

"I suppose we need to find out first if it's possible for him to be a monk. He said he wants to go to Darama... something."

"Dharamshala?"

"Yes, that's it. I'll type in how to be a Buddhist monk Dharamshala." She scrolls down a list for a short while. "Look here's something. It says you have to find a teacher first, one that has authority to ordain monks; and you have to study before you become a novice; and then study more to become a monk. It doesn't look very hopeful. But that was the answer to a Western adult's question. It doesn't say anything about how Tibetan children become monks."

They go on looking for a while and then Betty sees some pictures of very young children with monks in a monastery. "Look, here it says there is a children's home called The Village, created in India for parent-less Tibetan children and there's an e-mail address. I'll send an e mail and see if they can answer our questions."

Angel of Eternal Life

Robin's lying in bed worried about Chris and his mum and thinking about Tsering. What will be the answer to their e-mail? Then finds herself wondering about the cycle of living and dying and being born again. She often holds her crystal when in bed. Lying with it in her hand, tucked under her pillow with her head resting on it. She falls asleep aware of the crystal in her hand and it's there in her dream.

Robin is standing on the edge of a plateau, looking out over a desert. Below her to the left are the roof tops of a small community, their houses look like they're moulded from the desert sand. In front of her, her crystal rises in the distance, as tall as a cliff face. The Suns' rays focused through the tip, like the beacon of a lighthouse. By her side stands one of the desert people. She doesn't recognise him from her usual life, but in her dream, she knows that she trusts and looks up to him.

He's gazing into the beacon of light that radiates from the tip of her crystal. Robin can't look towards it without shading her eyes with her hand, as she listens to him speak.

"Ah, the light of Eternal Life. I am one of the guardians of the Tree of Eternal Life. We are all born with freedom of choice. And that freedom of choice will always lead each of us to lessons; lessons that teach us that in the end the straightest path to peace can only be in harmony with the Eternal Law, through love. Truthfulness in thought, word and deed will place the soul in the endless light of Eternal Life. In living in harmony with this Eternal Law, we fulfil our role as keepers of the Tree of Eternal Life."

Robin looks around her as far as she can see. "But where is the tree? I can't see it."

"The Tree of Eternal Life is found within the heart of creation, at the point where all life is related, each to the other and as the roots of the tree mirror its branches, so life is created as above so below; as with the Angels of the Heavenly Father and the Angels of Earthly Mother."

Robin turns and there is the branch of a mighty tree and on the branch in her web, sits a seemingly crystalline spider. Her nearly transparent body and long legs are lit like rain drops in sunlight. Robin can see there are many more of the intricate webs, spun with slender threads of light.

As she looks, she becomes smaller and smaller and the tree and the webs and the spider become bigger and bigger.

The spider speaks. "Each web is an expression of the infinite possibilities of creation. You are an infinite being who in many forms will continue to weave patterns of life and living throughout time."

Robin finds herself irresistibly drawn to the spider's web, tracking its thread with her eye, following the spiral maze. Inwards and inwards, she's falling into it, the glistening threads turning eternally outwards from the centre. Until finally, there's nothing but the forgotten places of sleep.

Chapter 9

Chris

Chris is travelling by train on his way back from London. He's trying to hold back the tears that are threatening to burst through his chest. He can't believe what happened. He'd arrived at his piano lesson that morning expecting his teacher to be really pleased with how much work he'd done. Instead, he'd been told that his playing is losing its musicality and that he's over practicing. His teacher has decided that it won't be good for him to go ahead with his piano recital; it would have been part of the college recitals at the Barbican in London in the autumn.

Chris had to bury his feelings as he escaped down the collage corridors, passing smiling students. Out on to London streets and down the underground escalator; to stand rocking on the platform, hands deep in his packets, rocking from heel to toe and breathing deep, to push down the welling disappointment.

His teacher said it's not good enough for him to practice on Betty's old upright and anyway he's under too much stress. He's to miss his next lesson and return in two weeks' time, with a piece of his own.

He can't remember getting to the station and catching the mainline train. Now he's sitting on the train, facing two ladies. Thankfully they're occupied with their phones. He stairs out of the widow, avoiding the eyes of any other passengers.

Chris feels like he's losing everything. His mother's worse again and because the treatment isn't working, she's still in hospital waiting for a heart transplant. And now he can't give the recital that he's been working towards for almost a year. It had meant so much to him. He's afraid of disappointing his mother, worried that she will feel bad. That she'll think that it's her fault because she's ill. His practice was the only thing that was keeping him from falling apart and now that has been taken away from him. Surely his teacher can understand what it means to take it all away? The seeming heartlessness of it makes it doubly painful.

The train pulls into their small station. Chris is glad to come to the end of the journey without breaking down in front these strangers.

They rush past him as he crosses the footbridge, eager to get on with their lives. Chris can't see a life that he's in any hurry to get to and just puts one foot in front of the other in a daze. But then he gets to the exit and Betty and Robin are there with the car, all smiles and hugs and chatter and he's glad to see them, relieved to feel that there are people who care. He can't show it though. Can't put down his disappointment and yes, now he's wrestled away the tears, he's left with rage and can't help feeling irritated by their happy mood.

They're sitting in the car, Robin and Chris in the back seat. Robin can feel Chris is in a bad mood. "What's the matter Chris? You've been in the dumps ever since we picked you up."

"I can't talk about it now. You couldn't understand anyway."

Robin feels quite hurt by his tone of voice when he says this. She doesn't say anything else.

When they get out of the car Chris slams the door behind him and hurries into the house, slamming the front door behind him too, without even seeing how close behind Betty and Robin are.

Betty turns to Robin. "Now this won't do. I'm going to go and get what the matter is out of him."

Chris is in the back garden pacing up and down with his hands in his pockets, kicking away any of the smaller boys' toys that are strewn across the lawn.

Bobby comes into the dining room where Robin is standing and joins her, watching the others through the window. "What's going on Robin?"

Betty marches determinedly down to Chris. She has to grab his shoulders to make him stand still and face her and then there's a lot of arm waving while he speaks; until he's still, hands in pockets, head dropped, looking down as he rolls a ball about under his foot. Robin watches as Betty steps towards him and holds him in her arms. Robin can see Chris is crying so she moves Bobby away from the window, in case Chris sees that they're watching. When Betty comes in, she explains to them what's happened.

Robin lets out a shocked "No!" It wasn't true. Chris had said that she couldn't understand but she feels heartbroken for him and helpless, knowing that there really isn't anything she can do or say to make him feel any better. She's glad when Bobby stands beside her with his arm around her shoulder for a while.

The Mission Begins

It's a Sunday and Robin often has the morning off because there are usually WWOOFers around to do her chores on a Sunday. She decides to take Buster for an early morning walk along the cliffs and then stop off at Betty's for breakfast. Betty always treats her as one of the family.

When they're all seated around the table Betty announces that she'd had an e mail the night before concerning Tsering. They say that it is possible for Tsering to become a monk. The monk who would be his teacher will have to send some questions for him to answer, to make sure he's suitable. He'll have to get permission from his father; and they'll have to pay for his flight; and really, they should make a donation to the monastery, if they can; and ideally find him a sponsor and Social Services will need all kinds of procedures and paper work.

The children all agree that it sounds a lot more difficult than they had imagined.

Betty's response is. "Well, I'll deal with his father and Social Services and the monastery and you lot had better start thinking of ways to raise money."

Leaving Robin and Chris, Tsering, Aaron and Bobby speechless.

Chris steps in first. "OK, why don't we each spend three days thinking of ideas and then get together and share them and see what we can come up with?"

Robin arrives home and tells her mother all about Tsering and about Betty asking them to come up with ideas to raise money. They sit thinking for a while and then her mum says.

"Why not sell those little sculptures you make out of pieces you find in the wood? You can make some more and we can sell them on the stall."

"That's a brilliant idea Mum. Thanks. I can get May to help me with some ideas when I go to my art session with her tomorrow."

Robin goes to bed feeling excited about the next day. If she puts the animals she's already made on the stall, she might even be able to go to the meeting with the boys with some money to start things off. She's in bed, looking over to where the animals are arranged on the windowsill.

In the heat of the moment she'd forgotten how attached to them she is. They're a little family with names and stories that she'd made up for an animation that she had planned, but had never got around to. So now she's finding it hard to let go of them, but then she thinks about Tsering and her mum's right. She can make some more. She makes up her mind to put them in a box in the morning, for Mum to take with her to the stall.

Chapter 10

Angel of Earth

The rain has just finished as Robin rides Polly to the paddock. A misty kind of early morning rain that makes the grass bouncy. Polly's breath puffs out in clouds on the way, her back warm and damp and steaming, smelling of wet horse and hay. Robin leaves Polly eating fresh grass and enters the wood. The sky is clearing and the last drops of mist hang, suspended in spider's webs, dripping from the leaves in the sunlight.

Robin meanders slowly through the woods in the general direction of the village, picking up interesting pieces of bark and twigs on the way. Some are big enough to be broken into pieces and some are smaller, interestingly shaped or already suggesting a head or a limb or a wing of some creature. She left early enough to take her time on the way to May's and has brought a large shopping bag to fill.

This is her second art lesson. She met May on the beach a few weeks before. Robin had taken some paints with her, to paint the sea and May had come up to her and looked over her shoulder at her picture. They chatted for a while and when May heard that Robin was home schooled, May offered to teach her.

May lives by herself in a big farmhouse on the outskirts of the village. She had spent most of her life as an art teacher in colleges while her husband ran the farm but he had died a long time ago and now May rents out her well-equipped barns to people running arts and craft workshops.

The ground becomes steeper as Robin makes her way up Friges' knoll, where the trees open up into a small clearing, on top of a gentle hill. The crest of the hill is at the centre of the clearing. Across it all, lies a large silver birch tree that must have blown down in the storm they'd had the week before. Robin picks her way through the branches, eager to find some pieces of pearly white bark. She crosses a part of the hill where there's a badger's set dug into the sides. All of a sudden, she feels a strange sensation under her feet and before she knows it, the ground gives way.

She falls a sickening drop and the next minuet she's lying at the bottom of a hollow with steep sides. Earth splaying out from beneath her and out through the open side across from her. There is still loose, sandy earth flowing down the sides around her.

Robin's winded by the fall and as she struggles for breath she sees, out of the corner of her eye, a shape begin to form behind the curtain of falling earth. The walls of the bank are pushing outwards, to create the contours of a giant woman, formed out of the earth in the walls around her. Robin can't move. She holds a hand on her chest, still trying to take a breath.

The woman is lying on her side, with her knees drawn up, encircling Robin in the way that a mother might curl around her infant as they sleep. She raises herself up on the huge forearm that's closest to Robin's head, to shield Robin from the sandy earth that's still falling from above. Within the sound of the streaming earth Robin hears her voice.

"Shhhhh...." and the streaming earth becomes a trickle and then all is still.

Robin is still flat on her back, with raised knees, drawing breath into her lungs at last. She quickly casts her mind around her body ready to get up and run. She doesn't think she's injured. Then she hears the voice again: A loud whisper.

"Don't be afraid. Rest here at peace for a while Robin, with me, the Angel of Earth. Inhale the peace and nourishment in the scent of the good earth. Be as the roots of all trees and plants, held safe within the soil, protected and nurtured as a babe within the womb."

Robin feels herself drunk with an irresistible sleepiness as she listens to the words. The Angel of Earth's voice is so comforting. Robin feels as reluctant to move from where she's lying, as a babe in the womb herself. A wholesome, stress free sense of belonging and of unconditional love; and so she stays there, with her eyes closed within the embrace of the Angel of Earth, at peace, cocooned within the hollow of the earth, with the buzzing of insects and the Sun warming the air around them; drifting close to sleep with the Angel of Earth.

After a long, sleepy silence the Angel stirs and speaks again.

"I create all that sustains all.
Fulfilling the wishes of the Earthly Mother's generous nature.
To fortify all souls in their journey in this physical world.

I watch over the continual balance between plant and animal,
So that all live in cooperation and support each other's wellbeing.
And when each finds their true place in nature
And the whole Earth is your garden to care for,
All ills will be healed, through the wisdom of the healing herbs,
And there will be an end to physical suffering.

"Remember each time you sit down to eat, to be glad and to thank the Earth for Her great gifts. I do the bidding of the Earthly Mother who has given me my purpose, to nourish animals and men and to bless with fertility, that the Earth may never be without the laughter of children.

Invoke the Abundant Earth!
That possesses Health and Happiness
And is more powerful
Then all its creatures."

The Angel rests in deep silence and Robin continues to lie content within her embrace, the words still running dreamily through her mind. The rich smell of the earth surrounding her.

Robin becomes aware of the sound of a wooden flute playing in the distance and she drags her eyes open. She turns her head to face in the direction where her bag had been hurled in the fall. Half of the pieces of bark and twigs are strewn in front of it and as Robin looks at the pile of spilled pieces there's a stirring among them, as if something like a shrew is moving about underneath. But no. The pieces are standing themselves upright, like iron filings on a magnet and then, lifting up into the air they begin to gather together into small groups; and the pieces from the bag fly to join them; and the small groups twist themselves around this way and that. At last they resolve into miniature creatures, dancing to the music of the distant flute, a fantastical, fairyland, menagerie.

She watches, entranced, as several weird insects made of tree bark and the green-winged seeds from the sycamore, fly about her, crackling and clicking rather than buzzing or humming and a tiny stag with twiggy antlers leaps joyfully over a pile of loose pieces. The loose pieces raise themselves up and form a hare that joins the others, circling her in exuberance. She tries to catch one but they dodge her hands, still circling and dancing to the music.

Robin hears a dog barking. Suddenly all the animals fragment and drop back into their original pieces. A Cocker spaniel comes bounding into the clearing and races up to Robin, wagging its tail to say hello. Robin gets to her feet and takes a few uncertain steps. When she looks back at the hollow where she had fallen, she can still make out the form of the Angel of Earth, as she fades back into the contours of the bank.

A man follows the dog. Robin feels a bit wobbly but tries to look as normal as possible as she gathers pieces back into the shopping bag.

"Are you alright?"

Robin isn't sure what it is about her that makes him ask and is glad when he just accepts her saying that she's fine. She's not ready to talk with anyone. As Robin walks on, she puts her hand in her pocket and her crystal isn't there! She runs back to the newly formed hollow and thankfully there it is, gleaming in the earth. She must have been lying on it where she'd fallen and so she leaves the clearing, holding the crystal gratefully in her hand as she walks.

There's still the sound of music on a wooden flute, getting louder as Robin walks towards the outer edge of the wood and when she emerges through the last of the trees there's Tsering, a hundred yards or so away, leaning with his back against the base of an old oak, playing his Tibetan flute. The old oak looks out over the sea, on the top of the steep slope of the hill that rises from the back gardens of the row of council houses where Betty lives. Betty has bought hers and Robin can pick it out from the others, because of the large extension she had built for extra bedrooms. When Tsering hears Robin approach he gives her a warm smile.

"Hello Tsering. How come I've never heard you play before? It's beautiful music."

"Well Chris is always practicing down at the house. Any way I like it up here. At home I often played outside. I used to go to the river with Mum in the summer and play while she did the washing. My granddad taught me and Mum said she liked it and that it reminded her of him."

The Piano

Robin has only been to May's once before and because she walked through the woods this time, she comes in by the back gate. There's a large lawn, tidily mown, with a clipped hedge on one side. The other side ends abruptly in tall grasses under an area of young trees that backs onto the boundary of a field.

There are some French doors open and because May's expecting her, Robin walks in and calls to her. Robin is standing in a room that she hasn't been in before. It's a big room, sparsely furnished and well-lit with three floor to ceiling windows. In one corner is an elegant, gloss black, grand piano. Robin's heart leaps. Chris would love this. Robin walks over to it and runs her hand along the smooth, curved lid that's closed over the keys. She lifts the lid tentatively. Apprehensive, in case she isn't supposed to touch it. Above the keys, in confident, simple gold letters is the name Bechstein. There's a long strip of obviously old, green velvet, laid across the keys. At that moment May comes in and makes Robin jump and she drops the lid. It goes down with a bang that echoes through the strings, and Robin feels rather guilty.

"Hello there."

"Sorry."

"That's all right. You can look at it. It's beautiful, isn't it? Do you play?"

"I do a little bit but I know someone who plays much better than me and he'd love it."

"I'm afraid I don't play myself. It belonged to my husband. I should sell it really, but it's been in his family for so long. I just haven't the heart to. It was brought here all the way from London during the war, to keep it safe from the bombs. I keep it tuned and my guests always enjoy it, if any of them can play. Come into the kitchen and show me what you've been working on this week. I've some squash and biscuits if you'd like."

Robin follows May into the large kitchen. She shows May one of her little sculptures. One she had decided not to sell; and explains that she wants to make more, to raise money for Tsering.

"Well Robin this is really rather good. If you make more, I have connections with craft shops and galleries in this area, and with the Summer holiday season coming up, I think they could sell these.

You know you're going to have to make quite a few quite quickly to make use of the summer tourists. Why don't you ask your friends to come here for a day and we can all help? Artists don't have to do all their work themselves you know. Even Michelangelo had students who helped him and some modern artists design their work and then contract it out to be made, but they're still considered to be the artist."

May suggests they spend their time on the computer making a leaflet to go with the sculptures, to explain that they are raising money for Tsering. They phone Betty and ask her to send over a picture of Tsering and also use a picture they find of Tibetan children with monks in a temple.

A Prayer

Robin arrives home after her afternoon with May and makes herself a sandwich before going down to the poly-tunnel to pick salad for supper.

Passing through the curtains of plastic, Robin enters the poly-tunnel and is struck by warm, humid air and the muffled, pungent, edible smell of tomato plants. She squats over, working her way up into the tunnel, stretching across to pick the largest salad leaves. The irrigation hose is on, making a constant background hiss and dripping water sounds. As Robin makes her way further along, she becomes aware of a whisper. A voice: A whispering voice that's been in the background of her awareness for a while. She stops what she's doing and closes her eyes. The voice is still mingled with the hissing sound of the water, but more distinct with her eyes closed. The words repeating over and over like a chant.

"Celebrate a daily feast with all the gifts of the Angel of Earth"

Robin repeats the words while she crouches in amongst the plants with her eyes closed, midway through picking leaves. Her mind takes flight over the surface of the planet, looking down from a bird's eye view on all the Earth's gifts: Fields of wheat and orchards, vegetable plots and paddy fields.

The spell is broken when she hears Pete whistling outside.

After taking the salad to the house she walks up the track, to the stall, to see if she's needed there.

"How are you doing Mum?"

"I've sold two of your animals."

"That's great!"

"How was your day?"

Robin tells her mum how May thought her animals might sell in other shops and galleries; and about May's invitation to Robin's friends to go to her house and work on them together. She shows her the leaflets they made.

"I'm so proud of you Robin. Look what you've managed to pull out of the hat in just a few days."

"Yes, but it's all you and May really."

"No Robin. It's because of what we responded to in you. I like the leaflets, let's put some on the stall tomorrow."

They pack up the stall and walk home together and everyone comes in for supper with a hunger from the day's work. After laying the table, Robin steps back looking at the colourful, freshly picked salad and breathing in the smell of freshly made bread. She remembers the words she heard in the poly-tunnel and takes a moment with her eyes closed, to say them to herself.

"I celebrate a daily feast with all the gifts of the Angel of Earth."

At night in bed Robin tries to work out how many of the animals she should make. She's wondering how many she can really sell and is hoping that the boys have some ideas too.

Chapter 11

Prejudice

The children have arranged to meet for their fundraising meeting at the park, in the playground across the road from the small Co-Op. Robin and Bobby often spend time on the swings there, chatting together. The playground's about half way between their houses.

Robin arrives first and is waiting lazily swaying on a swing when Bobby and Tsering come into view. There are some boys on bikes a little way away. They spot Bobby and Tsering and head towards them, circling them menacingly, calling out names and taunts.

"Look who it is? A Mong and a Chink!"

Robin gets up and starts walking towards them, uncertain of what she can do but not willing to just let it go on. Then Aaron comes round the corner. Aaron has a reputation with the other boys in the village. When he first arrived at Betty's he'd been very wild and got into fights a lot and when he got into fights, it was usually the other boy who came off the worse for it.

Robin is pleased to see him. He's calmed down a lot with Betty's firm boundaries and generous heart, but he's not going to put up with seeing his friends being bullied. The other boys recognise him and can see he's serious so they cycle off.

They're still waiting for Chris. He's due back from visiting his mum so the boys start playing with a football while they wait. Robin doesn't feel like playing. She finds a bench and sits eating an orange and feeds nuts to a squirrel. Every time children laugh or shout, it darts away and back again. There's an elderly man sitting at the other end of the bench reading. Robin can't help herself. She keeps looking across from time to time at his book. The book is illustrated with the most beautiful engravings of Angels.

The man notices her looking and holds the book out for her to see the picture on the page that he has just turned to. "They're beautiful, aren't they?"

"Do you think they really look like that?"

He smiles at her question and turns a little towards her so that they're both looking at the picture.

"There are stories about people seeing them, going back thousands of years. Some are from scrolls written by the Essenes. They were found by a Palestinian boy in recent times. Hidden in caves in the desert around the time that Jesus was alive. Angels are mentioned, but I'm not sure if there are descriptions of what they looked like. I've never seen one so I wouldn't know."

"But do you believe there are such things as Angels?"

"Yes, I do."

"How do you know?"

"I think I know mine. There have been times in my life when I've had problems that I just couldn't find an answer to. Then suddenly a new perspective just drops into my mind. Just like that: Often in words, like a conversation with someone else in my thinking. A completely new way of looking at things that brings everything into a new light: Like a gift. Somehow I know it doesn't come from me. The first time it happened I had no doubt that there was an Angel whispering advice. Since then when it happens, it feels as if an old friend has visited me.

"Sometimes things just line up, like coincidences, but not; and I think my Angel may have something to do with it. Take today. I saw what was happening to your friends over there with those boys bothering them just because they're different. I was about to go over when that lad came to defend them. It made me feel proud to see him on the side of your friends; and the page that I turned to in this book was about the same thing, about non-prejudice. As I turned the page, I felt my Angel close by. It's a feeling that makes everything so quiet around me and I felt it then. Would you like me to read it to you?"

"Yes please."

He turns the pages back to where he'd been reading a little earlier and reads to Robin.

"And all shall work together in the garden of the Brotherhood. Yet each shall follow his own path and each shall commune with his own heart. For in the Infinite Garden there are many and diverse flowers: Who shall say that one is best because its colour is purple or that one is favoured because its stalk is long and slender? Though the brothers are of different complexion, they all work together in the vineyard of the Earthly Mother and they all lift their voices together in praise of the Heavenly Father.

He who has found peace with the brotherhood of man has made himself the co-worker of God.

> *Know this peace with your mind;*
> *Desire this peace with your heart;*
> *Fulfil this peace with your body."*

From the moment he started reading Robin found herself listening with unusual concentration, hearing the meaning in every word. "That's beautiful, and I see what you mean. It is strange that it's about what was happening right now. Things that seem more than just coincidences happen to me too. The other day I lost one of the chicks. I was worried about her and later on in the day I tripped over an old paint tin. It was full of used oil so I had to go and get some sawdust to help mop it up. We hardly ever use the sawdust so it's hard to get to, in a sack at the back of the shed. When I pulled it out the chick had been trapped behind it. She must have fallen down a gap and I would never have found her if I hadn't spilt the oil."

"So perhaps your Angel made you spill the oil?"

"Maybe." Robin's thinking that this might be just such a time: Could it be that meeting this man with his pictures of Angels has been arranged by her Angel? It does feel a bit more than a coincidence. But she doesn't say so. To suggest that they were supposed to meet feels too personal a thing to say to a stranger. "When you say you hear your Angel, why don't you think it's God talking to you?"

"I think God is bigger than that. I think God talks to us through Angels and through everything, through nature when we know how to listen."

"So, what is God?"

"That is a question that's been on my mind all my life and as you can see, I'm an old man now. To me we're all God. Everything is God. When you see the world it's not just your eyes that see but the you that is the sum of all the parts. And just as our eyes are one of the many parts of us; each of us is one of the many interconnected parts of God.

"When I was a little boy and I asked Grandma that question, she said that God is everything that's Good, and I know people will argue that there has to be good and bad, but I haven't come across a better answer.

"When we come across what could be called bad in nature, the bad is always innocent, in balance. It's only we humans who can really do bad and we always know that we are at odds with God when we do."

Chris arrives and the boys call her over.

"Hey Robin, we're going to go and sit under the trees."

Robin stands up from the bench. "Sorry, I've got to go. Thank you for showing me your book."

"It's been a pleasure. Not many people take the time to chat with an old geezer like me. My name's George by the way."

"Mine's Robin. Perhaps I'll see you here again."

"No, I don't think so, I'm just on holiday, visiting my daughter."

Robin leaves to join the boys. She turns and waves, just before stepping into the shade of a large tree, one of a row that runs down that side of the park.

The boys are already settled. Aaron and Chris, teasing Bobby, throwing his baseball cap over his head to each other. Bobby taking lunges at them in a good-natured way, trying to retrieve it.

"Hi Chris. How's your mum?" Robin asks, as she sits down beside him.

"She seemed a bit better today. She's been on some new medicine for a few days and she thinks it's making a difference; she wasn't as upset about my recital as I thought she'd be. I mean, she was upset because she knows what it means to me, but she said she'd been missing the days when I used to play my own music and she asked me to write a piece especially for her. I'm still not sure I can do it on Betty's old piano though.

I used to play Mum my pieces on our upright piano at home, but we used to go to London every weekend and stay with Gran. I'd have my piano lesson and then I'd spend the rest of the weekend playing my gran's 'baby grand'. That was when I did most of the composing. It was more like the piano wrote the music. It's difficult to describe. It was like the piano used to sing back to me as I played, so I heard the music in the sound of the piano. Even when Mum's well enough to come home, it'll be a long time before she's strong enough to travel to London every weekend, and Gran's too old to have me stay on my own."

Robin's itching to tell Chris about May's piano but recently no one can suggest anything without him becoming extremely irritated.

He says most of the time people say stupid hopeful things, or try to come up with helpful suggestions, when they're just trying to make themselves feel better, when they can't really help. There have been times when Robin could see he had a point so she doesn't want him to dismiss her idea before he's seen the piano for himself. She knows she has to find a way for him to discover it for himself. She's desperately hoping that he will agree to come with the others to make her little sculptures at Mays'.

The boys are satisfyingly encouraged by Robins' idea to make more of her animals, especially as she's already sold some and they all agree to go with her to Mays' the following week. Even Chris. He's normally too involved in his piano practice to take much interest in anything else.

They've been thinking about ways to raise money too. Aaron's dad is out of rehab. He's not quite ready to have Aaron living with him, but it's been agreed that Aaron can visit every Saturday and help his dad with his small business, cleaning cars in the beach car parks. Aaron says he can put in half of anything he earns. Chris, Tsering and Bobby have already got a plan to go around knocking on people's doors asking for odd jobs. They're sure that if they explain what they're trying to raise money for, they stand a chance of people finding jobs to do; and now they have the leaflets that Robin made with May, to help them.

The conversation ambles on, talking about pairing up to go door to door. Bobby and Robin, Tsering and Chris. Then they get stuck when they realise they have no idea how much to charge and will need Betty's advice; so they start sharing jokes and planning what to do with the rest of the day.

Brother Monks

Tsering is sitting back, watching his friends joking with each other. He's so glad that he's found these friends. He experienced prejudice from other children when he first arrived in London, and had begun to feel quite lonely. He'd started to think people in England were quite different and he just wasn't going to find like-minded friends here.

Tsering's very surprised and touched by the willingness of his new friends to support his dream.

They hadn't thought twice about giving up their time and money. It would have seemed perfectly normal for the people of his village to rally together to help a stranger in need. So why should he assume that things should be different here, just because he'd had one bad experience with the first children he'd met? Perhaps this is a kind of prejudice of his own?

He remembers the words of the Dalai Lama that his mother once read to him. That there may be differences in culture or way of life or faith in the people the Dalai Lama met but that he met everyone as human beings with the same human body and human mind just like himself. Thinking of the Dalai Lama gives Tsering a sudden thrill. If he makes it to Dharamshala he might be able to see the Dalai Lama. Hear him speak. Many people in Tibet have never seen him, even though he is their leader. He's been exiled from Tibet for so long.

Dreaming of Dharamshala, Tsering rests at peace within himself and finds a familiar place in the depth of his breathing where the breath comes spontaneously, slow and strong. A place in the stillness where he always meets with the brothers that he knows he will meet one day in the temple, where he is to be a monk.

They have been with him for some time now. Even though the dream has only just begun to look like it can become a reality. When he meditates he can feel them. It's as though he's already sitting in the temple with them. He's always sitting on the floor on the right-hand side about the third row in, with other boys. He never looks round at their faces but experiences that sense of familiarity with them that you have with the other children, when you're sitting in something like a school assembly. Except here they are sitting, crossed legged, before a shrine, lit by candles and lanterns, among many other monks. With shaved heads and saffron robes. Chanting mantras with the Om's in the deepest notes from some of the older monks. The air thick with incense, coiling through the warm red and gold darkness of the temple.

Chapter 12

A Gift

Robin arrives early at May's. It's Saturday and they all agreed to meet to work on her project. It's already sunny and when Robin opens the door to the work shed, she releases air full of the smell of clay and paint and warm wood. Dust particles glitter in the sunlight, streaming in through the windows.

It's a large shed. The right-hand side and back are for pottery with old, wooden workbenches and sinks under the windows. Along the left-hand side are shelves with paints and brushes and other art equipment. There are two blocks of worktables in the centre.

Robin pushes all the central worktables together into a long row and empties the contents of the shopping bag onto them. She spreads out the pieces that she collected in the woods the other day, in order to see them all individually; wanting to make sure she has something for the boys to do as soon as they arrive. She's so sure she'll be able to recreate some of the creatures that she'd seen on that magical day in the woods. She can see them clearly in her mind's eye but now, on closing her eyes, when she tries to recall how one had been pieced together, the detail evaporates. Maybe she's taking the wrong approach? She opens her eyes and steps back, taking the crystal from her pocket. Stands there, holding it in her hand and scans the pieces. Keeping her mind completely clear. After a short while she picks out the twig that must have been the antlers of the small stag and puts it to one side. Then she sees the piece that had been the wing of a bird and then, yes, that was the hind leg of the hare and there are the green, winged, sycamore seeds.

Gradually, she has small piles of three or four pieces for different creatures. She decides she ought to make labels for them so she puts the crystal down in the middle of the table and starts looking for a scrap of paper.

"How are you doing Robin?" May comes in through the open door and starts looking at all the pieces on the table. "Is that your crystal? I have something to show you if you're interested in minerals. Come and see, you've still got plenty of time."

May leads Robin through the kitchen into a study that smells of dog, with a slight tinge of smoke and furniture polish. There's a big, old-fashioned desk and books and a large wooden cabinet with lots of small drawers with brass handles. Each drawer is labelled in faded, elegant, handwriting.

May opens one of the drawers. "My husband was very keen on minerals. He found most of the pieces in this drawer right here on the farm."

The drawer is full of small ammonites. Some are sandy and crumbling, some perfect and dark.

Then she starts opening other drawers. "I still remember the day he found the first. He started collecting pieces from markets and shops after that. Here. Look at this beautiful piece of opal and this piece." It was a rectangular, pale blue mineral. "It's a piece of turquoise and see here? This is a piece of lapis-lazuli." The phone's ringing. "Bother, I left my mobile in the kitchen. You go on looking while I answer that."

She leaves Robin to open the remaining drawers. Each one filled with a new fascination; small clear crystals and amethysts, minerals and fossils. May comes back in as Robin is still exploring the collection. "That was Betty. The boys will be here soon."

She has something in her hand. "I'd like you to have this. I feel you're the right person." And hands it to Robin.

It is a slice of almost clear, dark gold amber. It's very skilfully framed with what looks like a knot from a tree. The bark has been taken off, the centre taken out and replaced with the amber, then sanded to a blond wood sheen with all the contours smoothed and still intact.

"It's beautiful, May. But I don't think Mum would like me to accept something as valuable as this."

"I'll talk to your mother if you like. You see, when you start getting older like me, and you have a house full of memories, you want to make sure that the things you treasure end up in the hands of people who will appreciate them. I get a great deal of pleasure and satisfaction when I find someone who is just right for an object that has meant something to me. I made this for my husband a long time ago and I wouldn't want it to end up in some auction one day. I think he would approve of my choice in you."

Robin decides she should accept it graciously. It's the most beautiful thing she's ever been given.

The boys arrive and they have a constructive morning.

Bobby can't really grasp the idea when trying to put the animals together so May shows him how to make bases for them from clay. Rolling out the clay and cutting out the tops and sides to stick together with slip. A kind of glue made from very wet clay. May says that Bobby has a natural feel for clay and he's feeling very pleased with himself.

Robin already knows that Aaron's artistic. He carries a notebook around with him and draws the kind of pictures you find in Spider Man comics and skateboard graffiti. They're very good and the wolf he's already completed is somehow more edgy and abstract than Robin's. She likes it. Tsering seems to see dragons in everything he picks up and has already made two, with long twisted bodies and open mouths. Chris hasn't done anything and nobody minds. When Robin mentioned him to May that morning, she said....

"Oh good. He can play my piano and tell me if it needs tuning." And took him straight to the piano when he arrived and he's been playing ever since.

It was such a perfect solution to Robin's problem of how to get Chris to discover the piano for himself. Without him knowing that it was her idea all along.

Angel of Work

Robin decides to take a break. She sits down outside, on the stone paved patio at the top of the steps, looking out across the lawn. On either side of her are two stone lions and out of the cracks in the patio walls and from beneath the lions, grows campanula. It's in full flower, a mass of low lying, lilac-coloured stars; cascading down either side of the steps and creeping up and over the lions, to drape them in lilac manes. Among it all is the incessant drone of numerous small honeybees.

The sound of the piano in the background mixes with occasional, friendly laughter, drifting across from the other work-shed, where a group down for the weekend are enjoying a printmaking workshop. Robin looks down at the amber in the medallion she has in her hand. It's like a pool of clear honey. The sound of the bees wafts around her in waves, louder then quieter as they sample flower after flower, tireless in their work.

She loses herself. Feasting her eyes on the luminous colour. The sound of the bees eclipses everything around her.

Robin closes her eyes, succumbing to the early afternoon heat. Surrounded by the relentless murmur of the bees, sweat trickles down her temples. She knows the heat must be coming from the Sun above her but all her senses feel it coming from the medallion in front of her and she can see, through her closed eyelids, an intense, golden light radiating out from within it. She's so strongly enveloped by it that she can't even bring herself to move, to brush away the bead of sweat that's tickling at the end of her nose. The humming of the bees settles onto one note and she realises that mixed in with the sound of the bees is a human voice, humming with the bees in impossibly long breaths.

"Mmmmm... Mmmmmm..."

Robin lifts her head. From the far right-hand boundary of the long lawn; where the grasses grow wild under slender, young saplings come clouds of billowing smoke. Through the smoke emerges a plump, middle-aged nun. She's wearing an old fashioned, wide brimmed, beekeeper's hat with the netting drawn down to her shoulders and carrying an old, tin, jug shaped kettle. Smoke streams from the spout, like an Aladdin's lamp. The nun is smiling and humming and when she draws close, she stops in front of Robin; the smoke billowing around her with the scent of rosemary and lavender.

She lifts the netting from her face and speaks. "Aye, we love our work, do the bees and I. You count your blessings when you have work to do my dear. The honest work of humble hands is the best prayer of thanksgiving.

"Be thankful you don't live a life of idleness where the day is without meaning and the nights are a bitter journey of restlessness. The minds of the idle are full of weeds of discontent. You know the saying; as ye sow, so shall ye reap. When you've found your task in life, you'll need no other blessing."

She stands, smiling her simple smile at Robin, as though she were perhaps simpleminded; or has some expectation of something that Robin should say in response, but at the same time something behind the smiling eyes seems to be calculating exactly who Robin is; like a tailor skilfully guessing at someone's measurements.

Then, quite abruptly she says. "I'll be on my way then. Good day to you my dear." And continues on her way, down the path that runs along the side of the house, and out of site.

Chris has stopped playing the piano and the visiting group have gone to the house for a break. Robin closes her eyes, sitting in the silence and mid-day heat, enjoying the scent of rosemary and lavender in the dwindling smoke. After a little while she opens her eyes and looks down again at the amber, turning it in her hand and a familiar voice speaks to her from within the silence. It's the voice of the man who had stood beside her when they were gazing into the beacon of light from her crystal, in her dream.

"In your work you become a co-creator with The Creator. Sharing in the creation of your reality. Use, with gratitude the tools that you have been blessed with, to make your own unique contribution. This is the joy of work. Give freely to life and be a part of life's abundance.

Angel of Creative Work,
Descend upon Humanity,
And grant Abundance to all.

And we shall labour together in the Garden of Fellowship."

Chapter 13

The Letter

Tsering sits crossed legged on his bed holding an unopened letter. It has just arrived in the morning post from India. It's the letter they have been waiting for. From the monk who was to ask questions to determine if Tsering is a suitable candidate.

He turns it over and stops to look at the exotic stamps. Then he closes his eyes and takes a deep breath and using one side of a pair of scissors he carefully slices open the envelope. Opening it instantly releases a smell that takes him back to the small temple in Tibet that his mother used to take him to.

His mother. The pain stabs through his heart. So much has happened so quickly since she died. He's been in a numb daze in order to cope. And now. Now. He misses her. He misses her so much. The feeling is so overwhelming that he loses interest in what's inside the envelope and just sits there, clasping it to his heart, rocking backwards and forwards, tears and snot streaming down his face. He doesn't care, even though he can taste the saltiness of it on his lip. "Who cares?" The pain is so overwhelming. It's like being caught in a fast-flowing river, cascading powerfully through a narrow ravine. How can he ever get out? Only drowning will relieve the pain.

He rolls onto his side, bringing his knees up and hugging his pillow, burying his face in it and sobs. The sobs just will not let him go...

In the end they do go though. He lies exhausted. Breathing heavily. Staring at nothing. Not knowing how to ever feel normal again. The pain didn't go away but became quieter. And in that quiet Tsering hears his mother's voice calling in his mind.

"The letter Tsering!"

The envelope is crumpled, tight in his hand. He slowly unclasps his fingers and sits up again and flattens it out, then removes the letter. The paper is familiar to him. It wouldn't be to his English friends. Nor would the script. Written in Tibetan calligraphy are the words. *Why do you need me as your teacher? When you know the answer, I will hand you the key.*

Tsering has been worrying about what the questions might be. He hadn't even been told what he was supposed to revise. Maybe they would be questions to reveal something about his character? But what was this? How is he supposed to answer this?

Tsering hears Betty's exuberant voice, raised in greeting to someone. "Probably Robin" he thinks. She's having breakfast with them and then they are all going to the beach, to gather bits for more sculptures on their way to Mays. He isn't sure about going down stairs. He checks his face in the mirror. His eyes are red and he feels self-conscious about how much excitement there will be about the letter. He knows they will all want to know what the questions are but now, until he understands it himself, he doesn't really want the others thinking about it. It's going to be hard for them to understand why. He doesn't want to be distracted by other people's ideas.

Tsering opens the door to the kitchen, everyone is chatting round the kitchen table and Robin is there.

Chris is the first to ask. "So, how did you get on with the questions?"

"I can't explain. It was only one and I don't understand it myself yet. I'll let you know when I do."

"Can't you even give us a clue?" Aaron askes.

"No not yet."

Tsering eats his breakfast quietly. Preoccupied by how different the question is compared to what he had expected.

Aaron gives Chris a quizzical look across the table and Chris gives him a raised eyebrow and a shrug, as if to say, "Don't ask me."

Tsering follows the others down to the beach. He is still so absorbed in the words from his teacher that he barely notices where he's walking until he treads on a piece of sharp, dry seaweed and has to hop on the hard, wet sand, while he brushes it from his foot. He takes a deep breath of sea air and looks around as the others walk on. Tibet is the highest place in the world, as far from the sea as you can get and the sea and its' ways are still new to him. The others are a little way ahead.

Aaron turns to Chris, "Don't you think it's a bit off, Tsering not sharing his letter? After everything we're doing for him, I thought we were all in this together?"

"I don't know. I think you could cut him a bit of slack," Chris answers. He picks up a piece of blue glass, shaped by the sea. Uncertain if he should continue. "He's been through a lot more than any of us. The other night I heard him in his bedroom crying."

"Did you tell Betty?" Robin asks.

"I don't want him to know I can hear him. We all need somewhere private. I just put on some music with my headphones."

"Hey, I'm just going up by the cliff for a pee." Tsering calls.

"OK we'll wait," Robin calls back. They are paddling in the shallows.

The place Tsering finds is a large indent in the cliff face partly concealed by boulders. He makes his way round the back of them. There's litter and shells strewn about amongst seaweed and mangled seagull feathers. He smells salt and damp rock and what he suspects is the smell of other peoples' pee. So he gets out of there as soon as he can. He turns and looks up. There is a cave about twelve meters up. The others are walking towards him and when they meet, they stand and look up at the cave together.

"There are caves like this in the mountains in Tibet." Tsering tells them. "High up. Very cold. Monks go to them to meditate on their own. Sometimes for months."

"I don't think anyone can live in that one," answers Robin. "It's too hard a climb."

Tsering thinks not, but he doesn't say so. He's used to climbing and has already worked out the handholds.

"We call it the Watchers Cave because Bobby once thought he saw someone looking out to sea up there," says Chris. "We had a look to see if you can get to it from the top, but we couldn't find anything."

"Hey, look what I've found," calls Robin. She has picked up a small piece of driftwood that already looks a bit like a man running on top of a wave. So they leave the cave and go on looking for pieces for their sculptures.

Robin and Chris

Chris and Robin are walking side by side, searching for driftwood in the line of seaweed close to the seas' edge. "How did your visit to the school go?" Chris asks.

Robin had a meeting with the Head Mistress, Mrs. Meltwood and the social worker Zac Christian, at the school, a week ago.

Mrs. Meltwood was a plump, warm-hearted woman. She seemed always on the edge of laughter when she spoke and Robin liked her very much.

"They said if I felt overwhelmed sometimes, I could spend some periods in the library with Miss Pagdon the learning support teacher and Sue the girl she supports. I like the idea but I'm not sure. It might make things worse if the others think I'm different.

"There were some girls sitting on a wall teasing each other, when Mum and I came out, she thought they were being really mean to each other but I could tell it was just a game. They do it to see who can give the coolest come back. I heard the older ones playing the same game on the pier the other night, when we were coming out of the cinema. I guess some of those are their older brothers and sisters. It's not going to take them long to find out I just don't talk like them. I'll always be from another tribe in a way. But I'm used to being on my own and I've still got you guys."

Robin knows this is the kind of thing that sets her apart. It's not really her lazy eye. They pick on that because it's easy and obvious. But it's not really that noticeable. She knows it's more to do with coming from a different background.

"Yeah, when I first went to music college it was really intimidating being with some of those brilliant kids," says Chris. "But I found out it doesn't matter if you're cool or not because what all the other kids are worried about is whether you think they're cool, and if they're like you, and not bothered about whether they're cool or not, they're probably the ones who will end up being your friends."

It made Robin feel so much better talking to Zac and Mrs. Meltwood about the ways they could help her with her problems at school. The odd thing was that knowing that Zac and Mrs. Meltwood didn't think she was being silly or that her problems weren't real, somehow made them feel less important.

Robin and Chris have been spending more time together. Chris's school has broken up for the summer earlier than the local school and they both have reasons to go to Mays. Robin: to continue working on the animals and Chris to work on his composition for his mum. There's something about Chris that makes Robin want to spend time with him, so she enjoys the opportunity to walk to Mays together but it's not always easy.

Chris is often in a bad mood, but when he's just being himself and his pride isn't getting in the way, he makes her feel like they are equal companions as they stride like two warriors down the lane together. They're not that different in age, although Chris would be in the year above if they were at school together.

Chris reminds Robin of a colt the Pempertons had. They bread racehorses and the colt had been bred from the finest and had stood regal and proud from birth, as though he knew it, but as he grew from foal to colt, they soon realised that he would shy at anything. There was a major event over a carrier bag and another time it was a car alarm. He refused to be led around the cattle grate and would nip and kick out with his hind legs with no warning.

One day Robin was leaning over the gate with Mr. Heath the horse trainer, watching the colt, trying to figure him out as he overreacted to a wasp that seemed intent on tormenting him.

"What do you reckon Robin?"

"I think he was taken away from Serenity too soon. I know it was the normal age to be taken away from his mother but I think it was too soon for him."

"All right then. Let's try him with some company. Go and fetch me Mirabelle from the other paddock."

Robin left and came back with Mirabelle the mule. She was a placid, peaceful creature. A few hours later Robin and Mr. Heath were leaning over the gate again, watching the colt and the mule: A tranquil scene under the Beech tree and from then on, he settled down and they were loyal companions.

They arrive at May's from the beach and settle into exploring the pieces they found, to see what they can make from them. While they're working together, they can hear Chris playing the piano through the open, patio doors. He's made quite good progress.

Tsering and Aaron take a break outside and Robin goes down to the pottery end of the shed with Bobby, to help him make the bases. She's humming the flute music that she'd heard Tsering playing in the woods and in that moment she realises that it would fit with the music Chris is playing. She starts humming louder to be sure.

"You know what Bobby? Tsering and Chris's music go together." She waits for Chris to start over again and sings Tserings' line, louder, more confidently. "It does. I must tell him. It would sound so beautiful. They should try it," and she gets up eager to tell Chris.

Bobby's instinct is to hold her back. "Um, Robin. Um, just wait a minute…" but she's already out of the door.

As Robin approaches, Chris is playing the same two chords, one after the other then silence, then the same two chords….

Robin bursts into the room slightly breathless and much too enthusiastic. "Chris, you've got to hear this. I think I can hum it. It's Tserings' piece. It really goes with yours. You've got to try it. I can hear it so clearly."

Chris is not in the mood to be interrupted; he was repeating the same two chords because he was stuck. So he was playing the chords, leaving his foot down on the pedal and listening to all the harmonics the piano plaid back to him. He thought he'd just about grasped what the next line of notes should be, when Robin came bursting in.

"What are you talking about Robin? This is my piece for my mum. It's not meant for any other instruments. Go and write your own piece if you can hear it so clearly."

Robin is struck full force by the sting in his tone of voice, the hurt disproportionate to the words spoken. She stands stunned for a moment then turns and runs out.

Bobby was behind her and heard Chris. "What's the matter with you Chris? You're always slamming doors in people's faces," and he follows Robin back down the patio steps.

Chris sits very upright with his eyes closed for a while and then slumps forwards with his forehead on the front of the piano. He knows Bobby's right. He just constantly wants to push everyone away.

His world had been so certain before his mum's illness. He was Mum and Gran's "Golden boy", on track for greatness in a safe world where he knew exactly his path for the next few years, and now nothing was certain.

He's also coming to terms with a suspicion that he isn't really that special after all. So he can play the piano really well. So what? There are people he can see around him who can't do anything like that but are much better people, he thinks. Much better Human Beings. Bobby's right and he knows it, but knowing it doesn't seem to make it any easier to change.

He can't find the key to change. Wanting to doesn't seem to be enough. He's never able to catch the moment when it happens, when his irritability gets the better of him.

He sits up again and starts thinking through Robin's suggestion more seriously. She can't know how much re writing would be necessary even if she can hear that the two pieces fit together. They might not be in the same key and he was supposed to take this piece back to his teacher, which wouldn't be easy with one part missing, but at the same time he's intrigued by the idea. If he's honest with himself he's not entirely satisfied with the piece as it is. It does seem to have something missing.

Angel of Life

The Summer days role on and they make good progress getting odd jobs from people. Once the word got out that they were raising money to help Tsering, people came up with jobs that they'd left undone for years.

Robin has arranged to meet up with Bobby at the church, to complete the job the verger found for them, digging out the nettle roots from a corner of the churchyard, where he wants to plant a tree. She's early, so ambles slowly up the lane. It was once the main road that ran through the village, slicing its way up the wood covered hill, with steep banks on either side, held together by twisted roots from the trees above. When she was little Robin believed there were goblins living among those tree roots. This lane is always sheltered and shady, not like the newer road, exposed to the sun and the wind across open fields.

The lane becomes steeper and narrower as it turns a tight bend and Robin's first view of the village is of an ancient stone wall facing her at a T junction; and within the wall, the back of the small church dwarfed by a very large, very old Yew tree, its mighty branches stretching far-out from the trunk. She walks round to the front of the church, through the small gate, then follows the path to the back of the church where she and Bobby have been working.

When she turns the corner, she stops for a moment to savour a little wind, cool and refreshing compared to the days' heat. She hears a loud "caw, caw." There is the raven again, swooping away from the church and towards the Yew tree. In the shade of the tree, she can see a man dressed in a white Arab thawb.

He appears to be performing some form of ritual. As Robin watches he's just stepping backwards from the trunk of the tree with a tall, glass bottle in his hand. Robin has almost reached him when, having taken three paces back, he stands still for a short while; seemingly unperturbed by her presence.

He raises the bottle and then steps forwards and pours water at the base of the tree and speaks the words...

"Hail be unto thee. Oh good living tree. Made by the Creator."

He steps three paces back again then repeats the actions one last time. By the time he's finished Robin realises, with some surprise, that he is the man from her dream and it's like meeting a familiar friend as he steps towards her and they stand side by side, admiring the majestic tree as he speaks.

"When Creation was young, the Earth was filled with giant trees whose branches soared above the clouds. In them lived our ancestors. In the shade of their branches all men lived in peace, with wisdom. In that time the trees were the brothers of men, standing patiently through time. The trees give, that they may live. They constantly give back to the Earth, sustaining and protecting all that live within them. They have much to teach us.

"We should love and care for the trees that grow in our land. We should keep and protect them so that they grow tall and strong and fill the Earth again with their beauty. The trees are our Brothers and without them the Earth would be barren.

"When you recognise the life within the tree and speak these words, then the River of Life will flow between you and your Brother the Tree; and health of body, swiftness of foot, quick hearing of the ears, strength of the arms and legs and eyesight of the eagle will be yours. Such is the communion with the Angel of Life."

He repeats the words again. Slightly bowing to the tree. His eyes closed and his hands pressed together in prayer with his fingertips resting against his brow.

"Hail be unto thee. Oh good living tree. Made by the Creator."

Robin has grown up with this tree but it's as though she is seeing it for the first time. Its bark is vibrant with life and colour. As she looks up into its branches, it seems to be forever falling forwards to embrace her. She's overawed by the presence she can feel within it. A being that knows patience far beyond her restless spirit.

"Robin." Bobby's calling her and she turns to see him coming round the side of the church with two garden forks over his shoulder. "Who was that?"

Robin looks back to see the man disappearing around the opposite side of the church. "I've seen him before and he knows me. I think he may be a friend of my dads'." She doesn't want to say that she knows him from her dreams.

Bobby has news he's dying to tell her. "Guess what?"

"What?"

"I've just left the house and Chris and Tsering are trying out their music together!"

Robin can't help the big smile that spreads across her face. "I knew it would work!"

Chapter 14

Where is Tsering?

It's morning and the boys in Betty's house are getting ready for breakfast. At last, it's the holidays.

Aaron is in Chris' room. Tsering can't help himself. He heard Aaron say his name just as he was passing Chris' door so he pauses to hear more.

It's Aaron talking. "Look, I agree. I've done the maths too. We're doing really well but we're still only a quarter of the way towards what we're really going to need. If we're serious about this, something else has got to come along that will bring in a lot more money and then, holding some back for a bike won't make any difference."

Chris isn't arguing with him. It's really Aaron trying to convince himself. He has a friend who's selling a good mountain bike and he could do with one.

"I'm sure the others will agree with me." Chris says. "No one's going to think badly of you. You've put in a lot already. Of course you should be able to save for a bike for yourself."

Tsering decides it's OK to open the door. "I agree," he says as he opens the door and flings himself onto the bed. The way he does it makes them all laugh.

"OK, thanks guys," says Aaron. "But I'll just keep back what I earn with Dad. I'll still put in my share when we do jobs together."

"Are we really not making enough money?" Tsering asks.

"Well, we've still got a long way to go. We're not going to make enough just with the ideas we've had so far." Says Aaron.

"It doesn't mean it's impossible though," says Chris. "We're not saying we're ready to give up yet."

Betty comes along the corridor. "There you are Tsering. I want a chat with you in my office after breakfast. Can you two boys take Bobby and go on ahead? I'll drop Tsering off at May's later."

The boys make their way to May's. Today is different. May has a job she can pay them to do. She wants all the old workbenches cleared out of the large, unused green house. The wood has woodworm so she wants it all burnt on a bonfire. When they get to the house Robin's already on her way to find May. She finds her in the kitchen drinking a cup of tea but she has her foot up on a stool, in a bandage.

"Oh no May. What have you done to your foot?"

"It was my own silly fault. I knew I was quite tired after preparing for next weekend's group to arrive but if I didn't repair the netting down on the fruit cage, it was going to be too late to save this years' fruit from the birds. They like to eat the buds before there's even any fruit you know. I just slipped coming down the stepladder. I wasn't even up very high but just twisted my ankle as I caught my foot between the last two rungs.

"I was very lucky. The man who's renting the caravan down there, Paul, he heard me. Fortunately, I'd driven down with the netting and tools, so he was able to take me to the hospital in my car to get my foot looked at. Such a nice man. It's going to put me out of action for a bit!"

"Have you got any help coming in?" Robin asks.

"A friends' daughter is coming in on Saturday morning to make sure the guests' bedrooms are made up. There shouldn't be too much for her to do. She'll stay and do the morning coffee and after that they get on with it themselves. It keeps the cost down for them that way. Do you think you and the boys can finish replacing the netting for me instead of working in the green house? You don't need to do the top. That will last a little longer. Just the sides. The tool box is still down there."

Robin meets up with the boys and they make their way to the vegetable gardens. There are only a few small beds in use. It had once been a much larger plot. When they look at the netting on the fruit cage it's all finished. Including the roof and the door and even some of the upright posts have been replaced by the looks of them. There's a man with a beard sitting outside the caravan with a kettle on a small fire. He smiles and waves to them.

Bobby offers to go back up to tell May about the fruit cage and to let her know that they will get on with the green house instead.

They finish their job for May and are all back at Betty's in time for tea, only tea is very easily forgotten when Betty realises that Tsering is not with them!

Betty sits down with her hand on her heart. "But I dropped him off at May's at about 11.00!"

Earlier that day Betty had held Tsering back because she had to tell him that his father had not agreed to him going to Dharamshala. His father had been held in prison while he waited for his trial, so when the judge gave him his sentence, he had already served most of it and now he was out on parole. He wanted Tsering with him. Social Services told her that he believed he had a reason to keep his life on track with Tsering to look after. He would have to find a suitable place for them to live. In the meantime, he had found somewhere for himself temporarily, near Tsering, so that they would be able to have regular visits at the Children's Centre.

Tsering responded with absolute silence. Betty didn't feel that she knew him well enough yet, to even begin to understand what he was thinking. So she allowed him to go to his room by himself. He was there for about an hour and then came to find her, to ask if she'd drive him to May's to be with the others. She took it as a good sign.

When they got there, May told them how to get to the vegetable garden but it was a mud track with a lot of bumps and potholes, so instead of driving down Betty allowed Tsering to walk down and find the others by himself. Now she pictures him walking down the track and longs to run after him to bring him back to her.

"I'm going to have to call the police. It's my duty of care. While I do that, can all of you search here, just to be sure he didn't come back. Then we must go straight to May's and look everywhere for him."

When they arrive at May's the police are just arriving too. Robin recognises the policeman who took her home when she ran away.

He comes up to the children. "Can any of you think of any places that would be familiar to him?"

"He likes to go up to the woods," suggests Robin. "I remember seeing him near the old oak, at the edge of the wood, on top of the hill behind Sea View Road."

"And he knows the park near the Co Op," suggests Bobby.

"What about the beach?" asks Chris.

"Yes, we've got that covered. The tide's turned so we've already sent a helicopter up, to make sure he doesn't get cut off somewhere," the policeman answers. He goes to his car to answer a call on the radio.

The children search and search at May's, there are so many places to look. If he didn't want to be found he could so easily be hiding.

Robin decides to go back down to where they'd been working in the green house. There are unused sheds down there. When they first started searching, they'd been very noisy, calling out his name. She thinks if she goes by herself, very quietly, she might be able to catch him out if he's hiding down there. It's getting late and she's very worried for him. Before she gets there, she meets the man from the caravan.

"Has something happened? I saw the police car?" he asks.

"A boy has run away. We're all looking for him. Have you seen any one since we left?"

"No, I'm afraid not. I'll go up and ask if I can be of any help." He goes on up and she goes on down.

There's a small shed behind the caravan so she decides to look there first. As she creeps around it, she instinctively looks through the caravan window. She stops, surprised and confused. On the pull-out table inside the caravan is a picture of Tsering! Robin turns and runs as fast as she can back up the track. The man is just approaching the police car and Betty is on her way there too.

Robin catches up with her. "I think that's Tsering's dad. I just saw a photo of Tsering in his caravan."

The man is now heading towards Robin and Betty.

"It's Paul, isn't it?" Betty says to him.

"Yes, what happened?"

"It's Tsering. I'm Betty, his foster carer. I had to tell him that you hadn't agreed to him going to Dharamshala. I'm very sorry."

"I told his social worker it needed to come from me but she just wouldn't listen." He sits on the ground with his head in his hands. "This is such a mess. Where can he be?"

Betty wants to say more to him but she's impatient to go on looking. "Aaron, I want you to come in the police car to the woods with me. You know those woods better than any of us. The rest of you keep looking here in case he's hiding."

Robin's standing beside Paul who's still sitting with his head in his hands. She puts her hand on his shoulder. She doesn't think she can be much comfort to an adult but he looks so sad.

"You're a kind girl. But he's going to hate me. I was hoping I'd get a chance to explain before he found out. Talk it through with him. He did this before: In Tibet, when he found out he was going to have to leave his family there. It was his Grandmother who guessed that he'd run away to a hermit cave.

"I couldn't believe he could climb up to it. If there'd been a hermit there, they would have needed a rope ladder."

"I know where he is! He's in the Watchers' cave. But the tide will be really far in by now." Robin hadn't considered it because to them it seemed an impossible climb. She calls over to Chris. "Chris, how do we get to where the Watchers cave is from the top of the cliffs? I think that's where he is."

"I'll have to show you. I can't describe it."

Paul goes over to May's car. "We'll have to take May's car. The keys are still in it."

They drive back down to the caravan first to pick up Paul's climbing ropes while Chris calls Betty, to tell her that they've thought of somewhere else.

On the way up the track, they see Bobby.

"Stop, stop. We have to bring Bobby with us" cries Robin. And they bundle him into the car and rush off.

The Wisdom of Ages

Betty dropped Tsering off that morning and he made his way down the track to find his friends. It was down a slight hill and he could see the others before they could see him. Once he'd seen them, he couldn't bring himself to go on. He felt so responsible for everything going wrong. He couldn't face them. Not so long ago, everything had felt so sure. Now, despite all their efforts they weren't raising enough money; his father didn't want to give his permission for Tsering to go to India anymore; and he hadn't found the answer to his teacher's question. He had been avoiding it and days and days had slipped by without sending a reply, and now everything was going wrong and he was sure that was why. He turned away, ashamed. He knew where he had to go. He must go to the cave and not leave until he had the answer.

Tsering doesn't find it hard to climb compared to climbs he's made before. But the last haul over the lip of the cave is a higher reach than it looked from the beach. He only just has the arm strength to pull himself over the threshold. He's shaking with exertion as he rolls into it and stands up, brushing dirt from grazed elbows.

The cave is about three metres high and goes quite far back. It's almost divided in two by a long, narrow boulder. The narrowest face ends about four meters from the mouth of the cave, with some large stones in front of it. It looks out towards the sea and he can tell that at certain times of day the boulder might be visible from the beach and perhaps that was why Bobby thought a person was standing there. It makes a comfortable back rest when Tsering sits on one of the stones to meditate.

Now is the time to still his mind. He's full of agitation. What was it that his uncle had taught him? Not to fight it. To allow it: To sit with it. It's hard. He thinks he's settled and then his mind fills with doubts and reasons to feel sorry for himself, and reasons to be angry, but also something that makes the experience of the next second of sitting, doing nothing unbearable. "What is that?" He remembers his uncles' words again.

"Just breath. Follow your breath; in and out. If you get distracted it's not important. Just bring your attention back to your breath, keeping your mind alert and clear."

OK, he can do that. He can do that.

He must have been sitting there for a long time because when he gets up to stretch his legs the light is quite different. He looks out of the cave; the beach has gone and the sea is lapping against the cliff beneath him. The other children told him about the tide but he hadn't really grasped it, hadn't imagined that such a huge body of water could move so much. It means he's stuck there he supposes. He has no idea for how long. He's not concerned. He's not afraid of facing time. He's in quite a different place and feels drawn to sit and meditate again, like someone drawn to the smooth sensation of a drink of water when thirsty. He sits and closes his eyes again.

There's the sound of a helicopter coming near and then back into the distance but it doesn't distract him. Something falls into place inside him and he finds himself transported to a dark temple. Resting within the temple, taking up almost the whole length and most of the space inside, is a huge, reclining Buddha. Tsering is standing beside the Buddha half way inside the temple. The dark wooden doorway framing the bright sunlight outside. Inside it's very dark, but he can just make out that beneath the base that the Buddha reclines on, are stored hundreds of ancient scrolls. He becomes aware that his teacher is with him.

His teacher speaks. "There are often times when others can see us more clearly than we can see ourselves. We can be fooled by our blindness. How do we know what we are blind to without someone to show us the way?

"I am your teacher, I see you. I am the one to lead you beyond the labyrinths of your mind.

"These scrolls are the words of the Ancient Ones, written with Wisdom flowing from their hearts and through their hands. Understanding what has been written creates wisdom in the hearts of those who study them so that we remember from one generation to another.

"Those who have no faith in the wisdom of their own hearts will turn these words into dogma, and then they become distorted over time through fear.

"All these written words are doorways to unwritten laws, that are too deep for words: Doorways that open our hearts to unwritten Truth. And in the end the key is always the wisdom in your own heart."

Tsering continues to meditate in a state of deep inner peace. The words drifting into silence.

"I am the one to lead you beyond the labyrinths of your mind. The key is always the wisdom in your own heart."

Beneath him the sea laps at the base of the cliff, carrying the words...

"Peace,
Angel of Peace,
Be always everywhere."

The Rescue

Paul parks the car. They have to walk the rest of the way to the top of the cliff. Robin's impatient to get there. The light is fading and she can tell that Paul is not going to wait for help, she's worried he will still try to climb down to the cave even if there isn't enough light.

When they get to the position of the cave, they can see there is a bit of an overhang.

"I'm not going to be able to bring him back this way." Says Paul.

"We're going to have to wait for the coast guard. I'm still going down to him though. I have a whistle. I'll blow it to let you know I have him."

There are some well-established thorn trees at the top of the cliff and Paul secures his climbing rope to one of these and is over the edge before Robin has time to catch her breath. Robin and Chris lay down on their stomachs to peer over the edge, trying to get a sight of Paul, while Bobby stands nervously behind them, but they can't get close enough to the edge safely, to see past the overhang. All they can do is sit and wait.

Paul isn't able to climb straight into the cave. He has to go to one side of it and climb down to a shelf that runs underneath it; and then approach it the same way that Tsering had. Because he's taller than Tsering he's able to see into the cave before climbing into it. Tsering hasn't heard him. He's still sitting on a stone, his back against the boulder, in deep meditation.

The sun is now low on the horizon and shining into the cave and onto Tsering. Paul pauses before going into the cave. He's struck by what he sees. Tsering looks so concentrated. In that moment he hardly knows his son. What he sees is a Tibetan monk. Some stones come loose under his feet and tumble down the cliff face into the sea, so he has to haul himself into the cave or lose his footing. At that moment Tsering opens his eyes. He's no longer the fully-fledged monk, but a young boy again and he goes running to his father.

"Dad, Dad. I've got it! I've got the answer to the question."

It seems an age before Robin and Chris hear the whistle. They're so excited that they'd guessed right and Tsering is there, safe. Bobby claps his hands and does a little dance.

Robin calls Betty to let her know that they've found Tsering and to ask her to describe to the police where they are.

The coastguards, then a police car arrive soon after. They settle a helicopter near the parked car. When they come over and look at the overhang, they decide that one of them will climb down to the cave to help harness Tsering. They'll have to winch him into the helicopter.

Robin and Chris watch as the other man abseils out of sight, over the overhang of the cliff.

The helicopter takes off again and hovers so near to them, the sound of the engine is intense and the wind from the rotors blows their hair across their faces, even as they stand a safe distance back with the policeman.

Another coastguard is lowered from the helicopter on a wire and they watch him throw a line to someone in the cave. He's pulled into the cave and then Tsering appears dangling from the helicopter with the coastguard. To Robin it seems too high up. She holds her breath until he's safely winched into the helicopter.

Once Tsering's in the helicopter Paul and the other coastguard climb back up. Then the helicopter lands and Tsering, Bobby and Chris are whisked away, to be driven back to Bettys' in the police car.

Paul wants so much to go back to Bettys' with Tsering, but he knows Betty can't allow it. Visits have to be arranged by Social Services while Tsering is in her care.

Paul drops Robin home on his way back to Mays.

To Robin the whole event had rushed by with such a mixture of noise and danger and efficiency, she could barely take it all in. When she goes to bed, images from the experience keep re-playing in her mind.

Paul disappearing over the edge of the cliff; The wind and the noise from the helicopter rotas and Tsering, with the coastguard, dangling so high up.

As soon as Tsering arrives back at Betty's he races up to his room. He finds the letter in his bedside draw and smooths it out on his desk. There's a space for the answer to the question. *Why do you need me as your teacher?* Ever since he left the cave, he's known the answer; Because you are the one to lead me beyond the labyrinths of my mind. But now, sitting in front of the question, he realises that he must give his own answer and he writes in the best Tibetan calligraphy that he can manage; Because you already are my teacher; and the key is the wisdom in my own heart. He folds the letter and puts it into the envelope Betty has addressed for him and runs down stairs to find Betty.

"Betty, I must post this now."

"Sweetheart it's much too late. We have to go to the post office in the morning and get stamps for it."

This is agony for Tsering. He won't feel at ease until he knows it's on its way. "When does the post office open?"

"9.30 I think."

"But that's so late!"

He doesn't think he can bear it; he'd been told by his grandmother that patience is a valuable lesson, but he doesn't feel like any more lessons, he just wants everything to be all right. When he goes to bed he can't get to sleep. He doesn't want time to question whether he has written the right answer. He has to hold on to that feeling that made him so sure about the answer he has given. But it's so easy for doubt to creep in. And he's worried about his dad. Tsering's worried about hurting his dads' feelings. This is the second time that his dad has come to rescue him. How can Tsering tell him now that he still doesn't want to live with him?

Paul goes up to the main house when he arrives back. He needs to give May her car keys.

"So, all's well I hear," says May. "Come and have a cup of tea with me."

Paul sits down looking rather dejected.

"And I hear you're Tsering's father. What a wonderful boy he is."

"He is wonderful, isn't he? I wanted to get to know him better. I'm here because I thought that if I had the chance to be a proper father to him, I'd finally be getting something right, but now I know I have to let him go.

"You should have seen him May. When I got to the cave, before he realised I was there. He was so still. I could have been looking at a statue in a Tibetan temple, and then for a moment the Sun flooded the cave and lit up his face and in that moment there was no more question in me. It's his destiny. He has to be with the other monks. I suppose he's better off if I give in to Social Services and let him get on with his life."

"That's not going to work," says May, "Social Services can't let him just go to India. No. You have to get him back. Don't you see? Only you, his father, can give him permission to go."

"Oh, I see what you mean, I hadn't thought of it like that. It's been hard to find a job, so that I can rent somewhere for us both. It's the main thing that's been holding me back. I've been willing to take anything but it's not easy once you've had a court conviction."

"Why ever did you risk doing a thing like that?" Asks May.

"I was such a fool to think I could make the money illegally. I just thought it would be the quickest way to create a home for Tsering and now it's made things so much worse."

May is silent for a while. "I've been planning to do up the Gate House to rent it out. I'm very grateful for the way you finished the job with the fruit cage for me and you didn't ask for anything in return. So, for Tsering's sake, I'd be prepared to let you and Tsering live in the Gate House, if you're prepared to do the work for free. We call it the Gate House but it's just a small cottage. It shouldn't take long to do and then, for as long as you're supporting his wish to be a monk and while Tsering's with you, you can continue doing jobs for me instead of paying rent, if you still need to. If you still can't afford the rent after Tsering leaves you'll have to move back into the caravan though."

"That's unbelievably generous of you. Thank you so much May. I won't let you down. I want you to know I really loved his mother. It was just impossible for me to stay in Tibet."

Paul calls Betty and tells her May's plan. "I don't suppose I can speak to Tsering and tell him now?"

"I'm sorry. I can't authorise that, but you can write a letter to him and drop it off if you don't mind me reading it. I won't say anything to him before he gets it."

Paul goes down to his caravan, looking forward to writing to Tsering. He has a wash and a change of clothes and settles down to write when a car pulls up outside the caravan. He opens the door and it's Matt the Coast Guard he'd met earlier.

"Hello. I'm glad I found you in. I'm hoping I can persuade you to come to the pub with me and meet up with the rest of the crew. I can give you a lift and bring you back when you want."

Paul hasn't met anyone since he moved, so he's glad of the offer. "Yes, I'd like that. Thanks for the invite." He reaches for his coat and catches sight of the pen, resting unused on the paper, as he closes the caravan door.

Chapter 15

Timeline

It is 3.00 a.m. when Betty's phone rings. She finds it hard to rouse herself from a deep sleep after all the events of the day before. She gropes in the dark for the phone and almost cuts the caller off by mistake, but finally. "Hello. Yes. Oh, that's wonderful news. I'll wake him up and let him know. Thank you for calling. Goodnight."

Betty puts on her dressing gown and goes as quietly as she can down the landing to Chris' room. He's difficult to rouse too, but finally wakes up enough to hear what she is saying.

"The hospital just phoned. They've found a match for your mums' heart transplant. They're prepping her for surgery right now."

"Wow, we weren't expecting one so soon! Thanks Betty."

"Are you going to be alright? You know I'm just down the hall if you're worried about anything. Any time."

"I'll be alright. Thanks Betty."

He isn't really all right. It's a big operation and they have been warned that there could be complications. Chris lays awake for quite a long time keeping his mind occupied by repeating over and over. "Please let it be alright. Please let it be all right. Please let it be alright..."

At 8.30 a.m.; May watches a police car drive past the house and down the track towards the caravan. She's very worried that Paul must have got himself into trouble. What will it mean for Tsering? And what will it mean for the plans they made the day before, to help Tsering?

Paul's enjoying a cup of coffee, sitting at the small table, pen in hand, ready to write to Tsering. He's feeling good about the decision he's made for Tsering and overwhelmed by May's generous offer and trust.

It had been an enjoyable night with the guys from the Coast Guard crew. They'd spent the evening encouraging him to apply to become a volunteer, and having slept on it, he's woken up thinking it's not such a bad idea.

He sees the policeman approaching through the window before he even knocks.

Once more Paul pushes the paper and pen to one side, then stands up to open the door. Cold dread creeps over him and he tries to compose himself. He knows there's nothing he can say. He'll have to go with the policeman to the station to find out what it's about.

At 9.00 a.m. Bettys' phone rings. It's the hospital. Betty calls to Chris and he comes down stairs to join her.

"They say the surgery has gone well and your mum's in intensive care for now. I have to go out for a while but I'll stay in for the rest of the day after that. In case there are any more calls." She calls up to Tsering. "Come on Tsering if you want to post that letter. I'm going into town now for some shopping."

Tsering runs down the stairs and gets into the back of the car with Bobby. As they drive towards town Tsering keeps taking the letter out of his pocket and looking at it and then putting it back again.

"What's the matter?" Askes Bobby.

"I'm still not sure I got the answer right. I nearly wrote one thing and then I wrote something else and now I'm not sure."

"What was the question?"

Tsering explains everything to Bobby as simply as he can. He tells him the question he'd been asked in the letter and some of what his teacher had said in his meditation. Then explains that he changed his mind about the answer at the last minute.

Bobby sits listening and nodding his head and keeps nodding his head with his eyes closed for a little while after Tsering stops talking, and then he says, "But there isn't a wrong answer. If the key is in your own heart, then as long as the answer is your answer it has to be right. The only wrong answer is someone else's."

Betty can hear them and can't help smiling.

"That's brilliant Bobby. Thank you. I want to go so much, but I don't want to hurt my dad's feelings."

Bobby puts his arm around Tsering's shoulder and gives him an affectionate squeeze.

Betty wishes she could put Tsering's mind at ease by telling him about the phone call with his dad, but she's been a foster carer for too long to make that mistake. She's seen too many children disappointed and let down unnecessarily.

Disappointments

Robin finishes her morning chores and clears up the lunch things with Jess, one of the WWOOFers. Jess is there because Robin's mother has a choir rehearsal, then a concert that evening and will be away all day. Robin has been to a few of their concerts so doesn't go to all of them anymore.

"What are you planning to do with the afternoon?" Jess askes.

"I'm going to take Buster for a walk and drop in on my friends."

Robin walks along the coast path with Buster. It's beautiful and sunny but the wind blowing in from the sea is cold, with clouds following behind it and the sea is full of small, white topped waves. They're quite breathless by the time they get to the top of the steps that lead up to Betty's gate. Buster's tongue lolls out of the side of his mouth, looking improbably long as he pants, staring up at her with a grin on his face and a slobbery stick at his feet.

Tsering's sitting on his spot on the front step with his chin resting in his hands, deeply involved in his conundrum. How to tell his father that he still needs to go to India, without hurting his feelings. Their arranged visit isn't due for another five days. It seems such a long time. As Robin comes towards Tsering she can hear Chris playing the piano and recognises the music as Chopin, a piece he plays often, but today his playing is slower and quieter.

"Hi Tsering. Is everything alright?"

"We've been praying for Chris's mum. She had her transplant last night and they thought it had gone well, but they phoned again and told Betty the heart might be failing and she had to be put on life support. There's a chance it will be alright but they won't know for at least another day."

"Gosh. Poor Chris. He must be very worried. I hope she's all right." She pauses for a moment thinking of Chris and then asks. "But how are you? We never had a chance to talk yesterday. You know I ran away once. Why did you need to run away Tsering?"

Tsering tells her the whole story. He tells her how he'd heard Chris and Aaron say that they don't think they're making enough money with only the ideas they've had so far and how Betty had told him that his dad wanted him to live with him instead of allowing him to go to India.

His dad has even moved nearby especially to be near him, so he's worried about hurting his feelings; and how he had felt that everything was going wrong because he'd avoided answering the question in the letter and now he thinks he might have given the wrong answer.

Betty's in her office. She's disappointed Paul hasn't dropped in with his letter by now. Is he going to turn out to be another of those parents who say things and then don't follow through? Does he really understand what it means to Tsering?"

A car pulls up at the bottom of the steps. It's Aaron's social worker Sarah. Aaron gets out and slams the door. He walks up the path as quickly as he can and shouts, "I hate him" as he pushes past Robin and Tsering.

He hadn't had a bad day with his dad cleaning cars until the end when his dad asked him to clean up while he talked with someone. Aaron completely overreacted. He'd been worried all day but managed to hide it until then. Sarah had told him that morning, before she dropped him off, that soon they will have a trial of him staying the night just on Saturdays for four weekends, before going home to stay for good.

All day he brooded over memories of his mother leaving him behind with his father. Taking his baby sister with her. Hearing the front door close after he'd been sent to bed. When his dad would go to the pub and leave him on his own. Then some mornings when there was nothing in the cupboards for breakfast and he would have to pick his way around empty beer cans and his dad snoring, still dressed and in his chair in the sitting room. Looking for scraps to eat in the discarded takeaway boxes, before going to school. But mostly he remembered that the house was filthy unless he cleaned it and did the washing and emptied the bins. He's still not certain whether his dad really misses him. Or if he just misses having someone to clean and cook for him. That's why asking him to clean up on his own, hit such a raw nerve.

Betty opens her door as he stomps down the hall and pulls him into the office with her.

Buster is bored and noses his stick at Robins' feet and barks at her to throw it for him. Tsering throws it.

"I think I'm going to go on now Tsering." Says Robin. "Would you like to come down to the beach with me and Buster?"

"I'm OK here thanks Robin."

"Can you tell Chris I'll see him tomorrow?"

"Yeah, OK. See you tomorrow."

In a way Robin's glad Tsering decided not to go with her because she wants to find Paul, hoping there's a chance she can explain to him why it's so important to Tsering to go to India and become a monk. She goes down to his caravan but he's not there so she goes on to visit May. She finds her in her sitting room with her foot up, watching the news with a book on her lap.

"Hello May how's your foot?"

"I think it's doing quite well. I just have to be patient for a little longer. I forget how old I am sometimes. It takes a bit longer for things to heal now a days."

"I was looking for Paul. Is he doing something for you up here?"

"Oh, sweetheart I'm sorry. He was taken away in a police car early this morning and I still haven't heard anything. I'd rather you didn't tell Tsering if you can avoid it. Of course, you mustn't lie, but I'd rather not worry him until we have some facts."

Robin decides to go home.

Chapter 16

Angel of Joy

Jess is in the kitchen. She's just finished the ironing. "I was hoping you'd be back soon. Can you take this ironing to the airing cupboard? Your mum said you'd know which shelves things should go on."

Robin carries the pile up stairs. She gets to the landing, turns and stops, takes in a deep breath and looks down the corridor. She doesn't like this corridor. Half way down there's a place where she always feels uneasy. Although nothing really changes; the light seems dimmer when you get there and the same wallpaper and paintwork seem drab. The air smells musty and feels colder. If you didn't know it, you wouldn't be able to tell, but it's where the newer part of the house joins the original old farm house.

Deep in her bones she knows there's a presence there. She knows it; and she knows it never does anything; and she knows it can't do anything, but she still experiences fear and has to force herself to go on.

The airing cupboard is at the end of the corridor. She doesn't like having to turn her back as she opens the door and starts to put things on the shelves. There's a steep stairwell leading up to the attic door behind her. She begins with the top shelf and when she gets to the bottom she has to lean over. As she stands up again, she just knows it. There's a presence behind her. It's invisible but she can feel it, standing in the shadow of the stair well, a few steps up, watching her. It has a bad energy.

Robin closes her eyes, breathing heavily through her nose, aware of the thumping of her heart. But then, in that moment, she finds something within herself that she hasn't experienced before: Confident and fearless she stands up straight, taking a deep breath and without turning around she says out loud. "I know you're there. Go away. I don't want you here. This is our house now. You don't belong here anymore!" And she feels a new sensation as if her whole body is expanding out from her, taking possession of all the space around her.

She stands a while longer, breathing deep and standing tall, feeling like a queen with no question of her authority.

Then she turns around.

She can feel it. It has gone. Gone for good. There's an ordinary corridor, in an ordinary house that's loved and lived in. She stays for a moment, taking it in; lets out a sigh of relief and satisfaction then goes on to see if Jess needs any more help.

After her tea Robin walks down to the sea. To her spot. It's very near their house. Hardly anyone goes there because the better, sandy beach is not a long walk away. There are steps down to a wide, concrete, sea wall. Further on are steps down from the sea wall to the beach. You can walk along the top of the wall for a bit of a stroll but not enough of a walk for Buster and the beach is covered in flinty stones and seaweed.

The energy is so powerful. Robin always feels strong emotions here and because of the currents there are often large waves. She sits on the top of the steps that lead down to the sea with her crystal in her hand. There's a chill in the wind that she feels around her ribs through her thin jumper. The sky's silver and everything in her view is coloured in shades of grey. She's worried, sad, a bit panicky. Unable to bear the thought that thing's might not work out for her friends. Holding the crystal with both hands over her heart she rocks in a wordless prayer for each of them. For Chris and his mother, for Aaron and his father, for Deborah and her mother and for Tsering and his dream.

When she looks up there is an Angel in the sky: A real Angel. Just like in the Christmas cards, with a halo and wings and robes shining with light and with a peaceful, friendly face.

It speaks to her as though it knows how surprised she is to see this form. "Would you rather I was a unicorn?" and changes instantly into a glowing, white stallion. Suspended in the sky, rearing and shaking its head with its horn, flinging its long mane from side to side. "Or a Cherub?" and becomes a laughing toddler with wings and a harp. Then turns back into an Angel.

"I am the Angel of Joy.
Don't be sad.
There will be change. You'll see.
Let the heavens rejoice and let the Earth be glad.

Let the fields be joyful.
Let the floods clap their hands and let the hills be joyful.
Joy is the reward when lessons lead to harmony with life.
The soul and the body become one,
To receive, with gratitude,
All the levels of nourishment, gifted, through physical existence.
Sing with gladness and be joyful.
And may all beings be happy.

"Call upon Joy with this prayer.

Angel of Joy
Descend upon humanity
And bring peace to all beings."

The angel sings a song with a strange music. Many voices coming
from one Angel, weaving lines and harmonies into the words.

"Drop down the heavens from above,
And let the skies pour down happiness.
Pour down happiness.
Let the people of sadness go out with joy,
And be led forward with peace.
Forward with peace.
Let the mountains and the hills break into singing.
Break into singing.
Break into singing."

All the time the Angel is drifting upwards and away, until there is
only the song, soon blown far away, into the wind and the waves.

Hope

Paul runs for the bus.
The police held him all day because he looked like the description
of a suspect they were looking for. He couldn't prove his innocence
because the only person who had been with him for the whole time
the evening before, was Matt.
Matt was on his day off, walking on the moors!

By the time the police managed to contact Matt and all the paper work had been completed and Paul was finally released, he was only just in time for the last bus home.

The bus drops him off at his stop and Paul spends the walk down to the caravan running through the wording for his letter, one last time. He's very relieved when he finishes preparing his tea and finally sits down again at the small table, to put pen to paper.

Sunday morning. Betty goes down stairs to start breakfast and even though it's not a post day, there's a letter on the doormat. She picks it up, so pleased to find that it's a letter for Tsering from his father. She has to read it and then she put it in her pocket to give to Tsering after breakfast.

Tsering doesn't know if his dreams are going to work out. He realises he's just going to have to be patient. That's until the letter's handed to him, and the calm acceptance disintegrates into excitement and worry, and he dashes upstairs to read it.

When he comes to the end of the letter, he's so full of love for his father. He longs to go home to him that minute, instead of wasting any more of their precious, limited time together.

Betty has good news for Chris that morning too. His mother is doing so much better. They've taken her off life support and are expecting a normal recovery.

The boys are in such a good mood they decide to go to May's together, to practice their piece, eager to play it to their parents someday.

Robin's at May's already. She and Bobby planned to work on the clay bases together, to catch up with the animals that have already been completed. Tsering comes bouncing in with Bobby.

"Robin! I got a letter from my dad. He wants to help me to become a monk! We have to persuade the judge to let me live with him and May's going to help us, by letting us live in the Gate House. And then Dad will be able to give me permission to go to India."

"Oh Tsering, that's amazing. I'm so pleased for you. I bet you're relieved."

"Yes, and I must go and thank May."

"How's Chris's mum?"

Chris comes through the door just as she asks this. "We heard this morning she's going to be alright.

We're going to go and practice our music so we can play it to her one day soon."

"Wow that's great news too Chris. I'll see you later then?"

"Yes. See you later."

While they're working together, Robin tells Bobby all about the Angel of Joy. He loves her stories about the Angels. She can never tell whether he believes her, or if he thinks they're just stories she makes up for him. But it doesn't really matter.

Deborah finishes serving coffee to the weekend group and stacks the dishwasher for May. She has a bit of time before her dad's due to pick her up, so she leaves the house through the side door, planning to read her book outside, on the lawn. The windows of the piano room are open and she's captivated by the music she hears. She peaks in through a window and can't believe how young the boys are. Everyone seems to know Bobby but Deborah hasn't met Robins' other friends before. She stays close to the window listening, with her eyes closed, leaning against the sun-warmed wall, until she hears the sound of tyres on gravel. Her father's coming down the drive. She meets him as he's getting out of his car.

"Dad, you must come and hear these boys. Quick, before they stop playing."

She leads him through the house and they stand listening with the door a little open, until the boys stop playing and then Deborah's father goes in and introduces himself and asks them to play the piece again.

Robin is getting stiff standing at the table, leaning over and rolling clay for Bobby. He's cutting it into strips to make into boxes. She stands up straight with her hands on her hips and stretches her back and rolls her head around a couple of times. "We're getting a bit low on clay. I better go and find May and ask which clay we can use next."

She goes into the house through the side door that leads directly into the kitchen. May and Deborah and Deborah's dad and the boys are sitting round the kitchen table. There's excitement in the air. A few of the leaflets Robin and May made are on the table. Robin had no idea that Deborah knows May, so she's very surprised to see her there with her father.

"Robin. Come and join us," he says, when he sees her. "I hear you had quite a lot to do with this wonderful music of theirs."

Robin blushes and sits on the bench next to Deborah.

He continues, "I was explaining that my job is to organise events. Recently I've been organising the launch of a hotel, for a brother and sister who inherited it. They've turned it into a health spa. I've been feeling it could do with an appropriate focus point and some entertainment. A fundraiser for Tsering's dream and this wonderful music would fit perfectly. There's still the opportunity to promote it." He turns to Chris. "I don't suppose you have any more pieces do you? It would be good to make the performance last a bit longer."

"I do have a classical piece that I've been working on for a recital."

"Yes, perfect. It's a bit short notice. You'll be performing near the end of the holidays, in about a month's time. Do you think you can have it ready by then? As well as this piece with Tsering?"

"Oh yes, no problem."

Chris and Tsering exchange a reticent look as Deborah's dad turns to Robin.

"Of course, we'll find a way for you all to come. I'll hire a mini bus. You're all part of the story."

Moving Forward

Aaron and his dad finish their work at the beach car park and head off home with Aaron's social worker Sarah, in her car. His dad opens the door and it's like walking into a new flat. Every-where's freshly painted. Dad shows him his room. "I got them to paint it white, so it'll be easier for you to paint it the colour you want, when you come home for good."

"I'll be off then. You OK Aaron?"

"Yes, thanks Sarah. By."

Aaron's dad goes into the kitchen and puts the kettle on. Aaron watches him from the doorway.

"Go on, make yourself at home. We got Sky TV now. I got a second job cleaning at Sandy's Sandwich Cafe, so we can afford it now. I'll make the tea."

Aaron goes into the sitting room. In the past, whenever he remembered that Lazy Boy chair that Dad used to sit in, smelling of beer and cigarettes, he got a dreadful, sinking feeling in his stomach.

He sees, with relief, that it's no longer there. He recognises the rest of the furniture. It looks a lot cleaner and there's a new TV. He starts flipping through the endless menu.

A little while later Dad comes in with two plates and puts them down on the coffee table. Burger, oven chips and peas.

"You eat those peas now. They told me I have to give you veg each meal. They're good for you."

Aaron can't help smiling at this, he always did the cooking for his dad before and often helps Betty prepare the meals and he likes vegetables and salads. He's even thinking of becoming a chef. He can't help feeling he's going to miss the kitchen at Bettys'. Helping her with the evening meal. Playfully joking with each other as they work.

The following morning Aaron wakes up to the smell of toast. His dad brings in a cup of tea. "I'm not doing this every day, mind. Just a treat, 'cos this weekend's a bit special. I can't believe it's your first weekend back home. There's a present outside for you when you're up."

When Aaron's up, having breakfast his dad's so impatient for him to see his present, he just can't wait any longer, so he rushes Aaron from the table with his toast still in his hand. Outside the back door, in the small courtyard, is a mountain bike.

"Dad it's the one I wanted!"

"And this one's brand new!"

"How did you manage it?"

"You see, every week I've been puttin' away the money that I would have spent on the drink. They said it would help me give it up. They were right. There's still some money left for a rainy day. I figured it should go to you. You've earned it, putting up with me all that time. It drove your mum away and I'm so lucky to have you back. Do you think you can ever forgive me?"

Aaron has tears running down his face. His dad steps towards him with his arms open. "Come 'ere boy," and wraps his arms around his son.

Robin doesn't feel she needs to make more of their little animals. They've sold plenty in the shops and those they have left, Richard, Deborah's dad, wants to have at the event. She still visits May once a week, for her art session and likes listening to Chris and Tsering practice.

There's quite enough to do at home with new chicks and two new kids in the goat family. Bobby likes to come over to help her.

Deborah went back to London for a few days and then came back with some cousins. Robin doesn't see much of them because they spend most of their time sightseeing, but a couple of times she ran into them at the beach.

The most significant event was when Paul went to the scheduled hearing with the Judge about Tsering, and with May's help he got Tsering back. It all seemed to happen overnight, once a Judge had decided it. So a month went by surprisingly quickly.

Chapter 17

Heavenly Father and the Earthly Mother

The day before the opening. Richard has hired a mini bus to take them to the hotel. Tomorrow, Paul will drive May and Chris's mother Mary, for the evenings' dinner and performance. Robin's mum Rita and Betty are coming with them today. Betty has arranged for Stan and Ted to look after the other boys. Aaron is with them, but his dad's working.

They set off early in the morning. Everyone's very excited. Tsering and Chris, very nervous. Tsering's sitting quietly in his own world. No one else seems to have noticed, but he never received an answer from his teacher. He's worried that all this is happening and no one's questioning if he's going to be accepted into the monastery. What if he isn't? He feels a bit panicked and embarrassed by the thought. Tsering remembers that day, when he changed his mind about the answer to the question, just before he wrote it down. He'd felt so confident that that was what his teacher meant, about the wisdom in his own heart, but he hasn't heard back. He remembers what Bobby said to him in the car on his way to post the letter. Then he feels all right again for a while, but the doubt creeps back in so he spends most of the journey trying to expel the worry from his mind and to remain calm.

Richard has to stop off in Glastonbury on the way. He's organising an event in the Abbey. Everyone's happy for the break in the journey. The adults want to visit the Abbey; the boys are happy to spend time at the skate park and Deborah went online and found out about an exhibit of clothes made from re cycled materials, in the Zig Zag building, not far from the skate park. They're all going to meet up for tea at the Red Brick Building. Betty and Rita want to visit Bride's Mound, which is not far away either, so they draw the girls a map and agree to meet there, a little before tea time.

When they arrive at the Zig Zag building Robin is struck by the freedom of creativity everywhere. The building is still only half renovated.

There are huge open floor spaces and windows on all sides, letting in floods of light under the Zig Zag roof.

They can see that people are living there, contributing time and ideas; some living in caravans, with an outdoor, home-built pizza oven and communal kitchen.

The girls have plenty of time to explore the building on their way up to the top floor, climbing the stairs through the bare concrete stairwell, to make their way up to where the clothes are on display. They're beautifully made, with autumn colour combinations; with splashes of bright colour and unusual textures in unexpected places. They remind Deborah of the costumes the fairies might be dressed in for a modern production of A Midsummer Night's Dream.

When they leave the Zig Zag building the girls follow the map they've been given. As they turn a corner, they hear a girl singing. They find her at the entrance to a field with her sister, helping their dad paint the gate.

"Can you tell us where Bride's Mound is?" Robin askes.

"Yes, you're almost there. We'll show you. I'm Roxanne by the way." She was the one who had been singing.

"And I'm Mia" says the other. "What are your names?"

"I'm Robin."

"I'm Deborah."

They walk through the first field, up a track lined with cherry trees. When they get to the next kissing gate Mia points to a hedge a little way ahead. "That's where our friend the fox likes to hide. We met him one day with Dad." She turns towards Robin. "I was ahead of the others and when he saw me, he just sat and I just stood very still. We watched each other like that for ages. He was beautiful."

"I have a fox friend too," says Robin. "I watched her in the spring with her cubs near her den, under the roots of an old oak tree."

They're on Bride's Mound without realising it. Only a small hill but such a sweet and peaceful energy. Robin can feel it beneath her feet and in the air around her. She knows that even if it wasn't known to be a special place, she would have sensed it straight away. There are young apple trees up ahead and they can see the Tor and Wearyall Hill.

There's still plenty of time before Robin's mum and Betty are to meet them so they sit in a patch of shorter grass for a while. Robin tells Roxanne why they have come, about Tsering and his dream to become a monk in India; and Chris and his mother and the music he and Tsering made together; and when she tells Roxanne about the other boys in foster care with Betty, Roxanne tells Robin about her little brothers who have been in foster care and how her mother has been ill too. It feels good to talk with Robin, knowing that she can understand.

Mia takes a sketchbook and colouring pencils out of her rucksack and starts drawing the Tor. She plans to draw the back view of her fox as though he's the one sitting, looking at it.

Robin and Roxanne are talking about the animals they care for. Laughing with each other about some of their chickens and their funny ways and how Roxanne's guinea pigs like cuddles, but only from her.

Deborah is quite happy lying, stretched out on her back in the grass, looking up at the clouds changing shape overhead, against the glare of the blue summer sky.

A small group of people come up the path and gather at the top of the mound. They have a fire dish with them and Robin and Roxanne get up and follow them the short distance to the top. They watch them start a fire, just using sticks of kindling. The woman standing nearest to Roxanne carries a sleeping baby, in a sling on her back. She turns and smiles at the girls.

"Hi, I'm Anna. Would you like to join us?"

"What are you doing?" Asks Robin.

"We've been on a workshop about the Essenes and we're performing a ceremony to say thank you to the Heavenly Father and the Earthly Mother."

"Can my friends come too?"

"Of course. Call them over."

Robin calls the others over and Deborah joins the circle but Mia wants to stand back and watch for a bit before making up her mind.

They are each given two sticks.

"What do we do with these?" Deborah askes.

"Say something that you're grateful for and throw them into the fire so that your words go out into the world in the flames. You'll get the idea by the time it gets to your turn.

You don't have to say anything out loud."

The ceremony starts with a man and a woman standing in the middle: On either side of the fire.

The man speaks first

"We invoke the Earthly Mother. The Holy Preserver. The Maintainer. It is she who will restore the world.

"The Earthly Mother and I are one. I have my roots in her and she takes delight in me."

Then the woman speaks. "The Heavenly Father. O Great Creator. The fountain of Eternal Life within our souls, who has made Light and Darkness and has stretched out the heavens with Love. Love that burns with the flame of Eternal Light and cannot be consumed." They step out of the centre and join the circle.

The next person in the circle steps forwards with his two sticks. "Thank you, Earthly Mother, for the food I have on my table every day." He throws a stick on the fire; and then says. "Thank you, Heavenly Father, for the love that I feel in my heart." And he throws the second stick on the fire.

As they continue round the circle the baby on Anna's back wakes up and starts to cry. Robin watches Roxanne as she turns to help. As soon as the baby looks at Roxanne he stops crying and smiles so Anna allows her to hold him. He doesn't want his mum to take him from Roxanne's arms, so she lets him stay there as they stand together, Roxanne holding him on her hip, swaying and quietly singing a little song for him. She's making it up as she sings, about the fire and the land and the people in a circle and the baby laughs and smiles up at her.

The young man who had started in the centre of the circle, goes over to Mia. "Don't you want to join in with the others?" he asks.

"No thanks," says Mia. "I don't think God should be split into Male and Female."

"That's a good point," he says. "The way I see it... let me think... Have you ever seen a film of a cell dividing, under a microscope?"

"Yes I've watched that."

"Well do you remember that the first thing that happens is that it splits into two halves? I think that's the first rule in creating this dimension. We just call those two halves male and female because they're the best words we have. God is still both of them, before and after the split."

Mia thinks about this for a little while and then she goes off and finds herself two sticks from under the hedge and joins the others. She gets there just as Robin steps towards the fire, speaking her words.

"Thank you, Earthly Mother, for all the animals and plants," and throws her first stick into the fire. "Thank you, Heavenly Father, for showing me your Angels," and throws the second stick into the fire.

Mia is last. She throws her sticks into the fire one after the other. But she keeps her words secret.

After the ceremony the group start talking amongst themselves so the children decided to walk back down the small hill. Roxanne and Mia's dad calls and they have to leave. They give Robin and Deborah a hug and they all hope they will meet again some time. As Robin watches them go through the kissing gate and turn onto the track, Rita and Betty come up the path. They join Robin and Deborah. Rita puts her arm around Robin as they turn to look at the Tor, each standing in silence for a moment together. As pilgrims in the past must have stood there before them, taking in that special energy that many feel, but none can explain. The energy that is Glastonbury.

The Hotel

They arrive early evening and pull up at the entrance to the hotel. It's a large, old, country mansion, newly decorated. Inside, is a well-designed balance between old and modern. They walk straight into an expansive reception area, with an archway on the right leading into a comfortable seating area with chairs and coffee tables and a sofa; and an impressive wide stairway, to the left.

Tsering stands, holding his father's arm, staring in awe at the scene in front of him. There's still a lot in the Western world that's unfamiliar to him. He looks to his left towards the stairs and notices Richard walk towards them. As he does so, three Tibetan monks make their way down. When they get to the bottom of the stairs, Richard holds out his hand to them and one of the monks takes Richards' hand in both of his and bows his head a little in greeting. Richard introduces the monks to everyone. Yoshi, Tashi and Kunjo. He had heard they were in the area offering blessings in peoples' homes to raise funds for their monastery. He's invited them to speak about Dharamshala.

They're about to go through the hotel, blessing it with their ceremony and they invite Tsering to go with them. Tsering's thrilled. He lets go of Paul's arm and joins them so easily. It gives Paul a small jolt in his heart as he realises how readily Tsering will eventually leave him.

Robin watches them leave, fascinated by the Tibetan monks in their robes, surrounded by an aura of mystery.

As they go through the archway, she notices one of the monks lean towards Tsering's ear.

"I have a message from your teacher," he says. "He says. Good answer."

Tsering looks back over his shoulder and waves to his friends as the monks move him forwards with them.

Robin can't help wondering what the monk said, to make Tsering smile such a smile.

The Concert

The next morning the children have free rein of the hotel. There are plenty of adults around, but they're all extremely busy preparing for the day. They use the morning exploring and swimming in the pool or playing tennis. Chris and Deborah play a serious match. Her graceful, precise technique an even match to his competitive determination; the others really only play mucking about tennis, then go back to the pool.

Open day officially begins at 2.00 p.m. and the car park is nearly full soon after. People are invited to look around the hotel and there's a marquee on the lawn for tea and coffee. In the dining room a stage has been set up with the grand piano on it. The tables are beautifully laid, ready to offer Chef's best menu for dinner, with one addition. Each place, on each table, has one of the leaflets that Robin and May designed. A short paragraph has been added about Chris and the pieces they are playing.

Chris is to play his recital piece first; Chopin's Nocturne in B flat minor, followed by the piece he and Tsering have composed together. They have agreed to call it Amma (the Tibetan for mother).

Dinner is a success and when desserts are finished every one stays in their place as Richard gets onto the stage.

"Ladies and Gentlemen. Thank you for coming to our open day for this beautiful hotel. I hope you will all agree that Andrew and Sasha have done a wonderful job converting it and that you will feel inspired to use all the facilities for your health projects; or indeed, to come as guests yourselves. We are about to hear these two remarkable young men play their music; but first I want to celebrate the achievement of these children. Robin and her friends: Aaron, Bobby, Christopher and Deborah. Come up here children. Don't be shy. Yes, and you Tsering."

The children are seated at a table close to the stage. They had no idea they were going to be invited onto it!

"These animals we have for sale are Robin's idea. As well as making and selling them, the children have been finding jobs to do for people all summer, to help make their friend Tsering's dream come true. They have raised enough money for Tsering's flight. With enough for them all to go with him to say goodbye at the airport. That's a great achievement in such a short time children."

There's a tremendous applause. One man at the back even stands up while he's clapping. The children feel a mixture of embarrassment and pride. They can't believe what has just happened as they sit back down at their table to re-join the adults sitting with them.

"Now I hope the adults can do as well," continues Richard. There is a ripple of laughter from the audience. "You will have seen the list of other expenses for which we are trying to raise funds. Please see me after the concert if you feel you can make a contribution. And now, I will hand you over to our guests Yoshi, Tashi and Kunjo. They spent time yesterday blessing our wonderful hotel. If you would like them to do the same for you, you will be able to speak to Yoshi after the boys have played their music."

The monk named Yoshi speaks the best English. He makes a short speech about how important Dharamshala has been to the Tibetans ever since the Chinese took over Tibet in 1950. How Tsering would not be permitted to learn to be a monk in Tibet and how the monasteries in Tibet aren't allowed to teach the children to speak Tibetan or allowed to celebrate their Holy month of Saga Dawa.

Chris is next on stage. To the other children he becomes a different person as he sits at the piano in silence for a moment. Somehow he completely fills the stage. All the clinking of glasses and the odd ring of a spoon on a bowl, and the whispering become silent too. Then he begins.

Every person in the room sits mesmerised. It's beautiful. Chris's mum sits with tears welling in her eyes. She is so grateful he has had this opportunity to share all the work he has put into this piece. When Tsering joins him to play Amma, the piece they have composed together, everyone is transported to a different world. At the end there's a pause. No one wants to break the spell. Then enthusiastic applause.

After dinner a lot of the people are staying the night at the hotel. There will be a band playing a little later. There are several people gathered around Yoshi and around Richard. Robin notices that the man who had stood when clapping the children, stays behind and talks for a long time with Richard.

Later that evening Richard comes to find the children. He needs to take Tsering, with Paul to meet Peter Ashcroft, a businessman who wants to sponsor Tsering and the monastery he will be going to.

Chapter 18

Autumn

Summer has come to flower and with autumn comes change: Everyone entering new adventures in their lives. Tsering is going to India; Robin will start school; Deborah, Boarding School; Aaron is going back to live with his dad (Robin will see him in school). Chris and his mother are going to live with his grandmother, while his mother recuperates. Bobby will stay on with Betty and they will welcome with loving kindness, the next child to come through their door. The river of life is moving on. And Robin must move on with it too. Older. Wiser: Her heart growing bigger and bigger.

Robin has a Dream

In front of her is the Sun against the full blackness of space. From far in the distance comes a faint cry. "Help. Help." Then again, "Help. Help."

A tiny sphere appears from behind the Sun. It's the Earth, beautiful and blue, the call getting louder as it coms nearer. Then it changes to the form of a woman. Curled into a sphere with her hands clasped around her knees. Turning in space. She has to keep moving her head, to prevent the space debris and satellites that are floating around her, coming too close to her face. Binding her is a mesh of microwaves and under that, a smog of fumes and gasses choking her.

"I can't breathe. I'm too hot. What has become of my beautiful animals? Where are my forests? Look what has happened to my seas. My beautiful corals. All this was made for you. Everything in perfect balance for your human bodies to thrive.

I am your Mother. I gave you life. Your body is created from my body. The air you breathe is my breath."

Robin cries out. "I'm sorry. I'll do whatever I can."

"Do. You must all do whatever you can. Your grown-ups have nearly left it too late. I need you. You are the last human children who can still have hope."

She's still calling to Robin as she travels further away on her path around the Sun.

"Remember. You are the last children who can still have hope. If you all do what you can, there is still hope."

Robin feels a powerful presence standing beside her.

"I am the living spirit that is the planet Earth. You are all my children. I need you to understand that I will always give with abundance. I can give you all that you require for life. All you have to do is care about me. Respect and nurture me in all my living forms and there will always be enough for your needs: And beauty beyond your imagination."

*